FEEDING STRAYS

FEEDING STRAYS

Short Stories by

Stefanie Freele

Introduction by

Bruce Holland Rogers

LOST HORSE PRESS
Sandpoint · Idaho

ACKNOWLEDGEMENTS

Grateful thanks given to the editors of the following publications for first publishing the stories:

SmokeLong Quarterly: "Arlo's Big Head," "Breathing Oysters," "In the Kitchen She Wakes," "She Doesn't Ask Where He Goes"
Monkeybicycle: "Tinfoilers"
Flash, Fiction Online, Get Born: "James Brown Is Alive and Doing Laundry in South Lake Tahoe"
Flash Fiction Online: "The Flood of '09"
Big Toe Review: "Crumple"
Hobart Online: "Sweet Venus"
North Idaho Lifestyles: "After Meandering Mendaciously Downstream"
Get Born: "A Glowing Pregnant Woman," "The Rain"
Six Little Things: "From Bootleg to Blackout"
Contrary: "At the Foot of the Mountain," "The Inexorable"
elimae: "Sisters"
Etchings: "Late at Night, Clever Men Appear in Your Living Room"
Spire, Thema, Cezanne's Carrot: "The Topography of a Wake"
Café Irreal, The Ides of Sandpoint: "She Appeared unto Him"
Downstate Story: "The Sinkhole"
Superstition Review: "What Came after She Left Him"
Wigleaf: "Because Condoms Seem So Desperate, She Also Buys a Fern"
Soundings: "The Other Side of the Diaper"
Literary Mama: "The Rain," "The Seven-Year-Old"
Pebble Lake Review, Frigg: "The Space between Two Sentences"
American Literary Review: "They Left Us Dangling"
Dogzplot: "The Many Canyons in Utah," "Every Girl Has an Ex Named Steve"
The Best of Boston Literary Review: "Kalispell"

Cover art: Michal Ashkenasi.
    Artwork by Michal Ashkenasi can be viewed at *wwwMichalsart.com*.
Author photo: Suzanne Karp.
Cover and interior design by Christine Holbert.

This and other fine Lost Horse Press titles may be viewed online at *www.losthorsepress.org.*

FIRST EDITION

Library of Congress Cataloging-in-Publication Data
Freele, Stefanie.
    Feeding strays : a collection of short stories / by Stefanie Freele ; introduction by Bruce Holland Rogers.
        p. cm.
    ISBN 978-0-9800289-5-9 (alk. paper)
    I. Title.
PS3606.R444F44 2009
813'.6—dc22
                                                    2009029648

I wish to thank the following people for their support, encouragement, and inspiration:

Everyone from the Northwest Institute of Literary Arts: Whidbey Writers Workshop, especially Bruce Holland Rogers, Wayne Ude, David Wagoner, Nancy Boutin, Susan Zwinger, Joe Ponepinto, Caleb Barber, Tanya Chernov, Jo Meador, Elaine Woods, Helen Sears, Robert Hoffman, Nina Bayer, Lois Brandt, Loren Cooper, Ann Gonzales, and Laurie Junkins. Christine Holbert, publisher extraordinaire. The Eggs: Pam Bolton, Laura Carr, Cynthia Beecher, Gail Larrick, Mike Kamrath, Nancy Norton, Corrine Meadows. Penelope LaMontagne. Adriana Schrader, who might possibly have enough love in her to save the entire planet. Kathy Fish. Dave Clapper, Randall Brown, Kelly Spitzer and the rest of the crew at *SmokeLong Quarterly*. The folks at Gotham Writers, especially Terri Brown-Davidson, Brandi Reissenweber, and Alex Steele. The flashers on Zoetrope Virtual Studio. Briana, Chris and Arlo Herrod. Arnold Rystadt for all those *New Yorkers*. Sammy Barbitta, my redheaded muse. Lian Gouw, Patty Meringer, Bill McStowe, Lisa Ventrella, Grant Hettrick, Kathie Giorgio, and Kathy Steffen. Lynn, Diana, Howard, and Bryan Freele. Jakob, Kali, Lucas. Jon Saputo. Keith "Dalton" Lewers. Jaya. James Brown. Sam Luikens for his astute copyediting. Seth Lewers for steadfastly believing in me. Our toasty little Wyett.

For Seth and Wyett

TABLE OF CONTENTS

INTRODUCTION

O nce upon a time, there was a reader (that's you, or someone very much like you) who was considering a collection of stories by Stefanie Freele, a collection called *Feeding Strays*. At this point in the story, I don't know what sort of character the reader is going to turn out to be. If the reader is a hero, he or she will buy the book. *Hooray!* If a villain, he or she will steal the book. *Boo! Hiss!* And if that reader is a villain who doesn't understand the economics of publishing or the penury of writers, he or she will try to cadge a free copy from the author. *Harumph!* Of course, there are those who will put the book down and not acquire it at all. They aren't villains, but they are guilty of a poor decision.

Which sort of character you are is between you and your conscience, Dear Reader. But for the moment, I'm going to assume that you're among the heroes. You have taken the risk, have surrendered a few dollars and some of your precious time to see what Stefanie Freele will give you in return for buying and reading her book.

Fasten your seat belt. At first glance, it may not be obvious that you're in for a wild ride. The world of Freele's stories is largely domestic, the world of diapers, mothers on the brink, men who didn't know that fatherhood could sneak up on them. But it is also a world of levitating babies, suicide vacations, and the earth opening up to swallow tractors. You will find stories of surprising brevity that paint a whole picture in just a few strokes and longer stories that build subtle suspense. Freele's stories range from realistic to expressionistic to fantastic and back again. Every time you think you've got her pegged, the next story will surprise you.

Freele doesn't write mystery stories, but you will find mysteries on these pages. Some are mysteries that the characters wrestle with. In "The Penile Bone," the word that Courtney utters near the end mystifies her. Why did she say it, other than just echoing what Sherii just said? Why was it, apparently, the accurate thing to say? Some are mysteries of character. How is it that the father in "Every Girl Has an Ex Named Steve" understands his daughters so well?

And some are mysteries of a very literary type: Just how is it that this story (or that one or that other one), which seems to follow none of the rules, is nonetheless completely satisfying?

It's the last kind of mystery that especially appeals to me as a writer. How is it that Stefanie Freele manages to write these weird and wonderful tales?

In a Directed Reading class I teach for graduate creative writing students, we read and dissect the work of other writers, looking for techniques the students can use in their own work. In the great tradition of artistic larceny, writers copy not content, but literary moves. This sentence structure. That method of creating suspense. We're looking for the kinds of technical tricks that jazz musicians call "chops."

Recently in Directed Reading, we read several Stefanie Freele stories. Students had chosen the stories because they admired them, but we found ourselves largely baffled when it came to analysis. We could point out a technique here or there, but the course ended with all of us feeling that there was something missing from our discussion, something we couldn't articulate.

What is it that makes a Stefanie Freele story so good? Why are these stories, which are so often weird, organic, and open-ended, also so satisfying? How does she do it?

Freele's stories remind me of the fiction of Ray Vukcevich. With both writers, I read with growing pleasure as I encounter not just weirdness, but the right weirdness. I've heard people ask Vukcevich how he writes, and here is what he says: First he writes down everything that comes into his head. Then he goes through and takes out the boring parts.

Oh, *that's* helpful.

In Directed Reading, many writers fall under our dissection knives into tidy, discrete pieces of writing craft. But Freele stories, like Vukcevich stories, resist dissection. I'm mystified by how she does it. Maybe she just writes down whatever comes into her head and then takes out the parts that aren't a Stefanie Freele story. To find out what that means, you'll have to read the stories yourself. What they have in common is a quality you won't find in other writers. They have Freeliness. No other writer writes with Freeliness. I suspect no other writer can.

I hope that as you read these stories you will chuckle, laugh out loud, nod with recognition or sigh with pleasure. May you discover, as I did, that the stories only get better when read twice, or three times . . . or however many times you go back to them.

Once upon a time, you opened *Feeding Strays* to the first story and began to read. Whether you bought, stole, cadged or borrowed the book, you were soon engrossed, and by the end you had acquired, like Stefanie's other readers have, a great appreciation for the hard-to-define, impossible-to-analyze, inimitable quality of Freeliness. May we all be blessed with many more volumes to come, and live happily ever after.

—*Bruce Holland Rogers*

IN THE KITCHEN SHE WAKES

She always comes to after midnight, sometimes in the midst of grating Romano cheese, sometimes in the midst of drinking hand lotion. This night, she finds herself brushing the edge of a mini pie shell with a mixture of lemon juice, zest, eggs and sugar. The counter overflows with the yellow spheres of lemon tarts. What to do with all these? 3:35 A.M. She calculates, by the appearance of the ingredients spread across the counter, she's been in the kitchen since 1 A.M.

She opens the oven to find four more pies cooking, one with a green rectangle half submerged. With tongs, she eases out the kitchen sponge.

She thinks she might call her first husband; he'll be up at this hour. He is always good at talking her down, getting her back to sleep, even though first he'd want to discuss why she was up, why she baked, why tarts this time. He would say that tarts symbolized something. She'd argue that if she knew why, she'd have told him and everyone else a long time ago.

But, Craig would hear her on the phone and get jealous. Again.

⌇·

Then she remembers that Craig left two nights ago.

The phone trills. Sammi next door. "Lasagna, quiche? I see you're light is on."

"Lemon tarts. Why are you up?"

"Menopause. Soaked sheets. Go back to bed."

"How many will you take?"

5

"Tarts? I'll take four. That's it. I'm not gaining one more pound because of you."

"It's amazing how they all turned out so charming. I wasn't even awake to check the timing on the oven. The crusts are a nice hue."

"Hue. No, it's scary. What if you put something else in the oven instead?"

Like my head, she thought and licked the bowl.

"Don't lick the bowl. The sugar will keep you up."

⁓

The moon is her only witness as she looks through the window. Craig's white truck isn't outside. She wants him to yell, "What the hell?" He'd say, "Get your head screwed on straight." He'd then wait fifteen minutes or so and calmly say, "I know you can't help it, but go back to bed."

She kneels down—the left knee cracks loudly on the tile—leaning her head near the four yellow orbs. The same heat that turns dough golden and flaky could disfigure her skin for life. She holds her head there, almost inside the oven until she gasps.

⁓

The motel manager patches her through to Craig. "What the hell? What the hell time is it?"

She can feel his heavy ankle across hers, that vein in his forearm, the damp hair underneath his hat. "It's me."

"What the hell did you bake this time?"

"Lemon tarts."

"No pen caps sprinkled on top?"

"They're perfect."

She hears him adjusting himself on the pillow. "I love your lemon tarts, damn it."

She can smell inside his glove compartment, cigars and tape. She can taste the shoulder of his wool sweater. "Will you just stay on the phone while I get back in bed?"

He breathes.

She turns off the oven, the lights, leaves the tarts on the counter. She locks the refrigerator, sets the alarm code on the kitchen. "It doesn't help now that I know the number."

"Get your head on that pillow," he orders.

She pulls up the covers. "Which side are you lying on?"

"Left."

"I'll lie on the right then."

"I might as well be home if you're going wake me up anyway."

She tunnels down, layer by layer. She barely wakes when an arm pulls her in toward a mouth that smells of lemons.

SHE DOESN'T ASK WHERE HE GOES

Years ago, before their son was born, she stopped asking his name. He doesn't call her during the day. He doesn't own a cell phone.

When he's in the shower, she opens his briefcase. Once she found hundreds of cough drop wrappers; another time, pieces of a violin. She has found many things: tinfoiled pizza, porcelain tea cups, dried sage, a swallow's nest, two maracas, a half-burned candle. She has never found a wallet, a receipt, a photo, a letter, a pen or pencil, or a woman's hair.

This time, as he sings to their son in the shower and she hears the tiny voice mimicking him, the briefcase holds three orange peels and a flashlight.

If he showers, it means he's spending the night. She makes the bed fresh, puts as many toys away as she can, pushes books under the bed.

The water is off. Tonight she won't have to answer, "Where's Dada?"

In the morning, three hundred dollars on the stereo before he leaves for work with a note, *Don't spend it on bills.* A smiley face is below his handwriting. Four swipes of the pen. One for the head, two for eyes, the fourth for the cheerful mouth. She puts the note in the envelope underneath her sweaters.

She doesn't know what he does for a living. He returns while the child is in the highchair eating curly pasta and beans. At shower time she finds a single palm frond.

⁖

In the morning he leaves cash to cover the entire month's bills on the stereo just like he does every first of the month. A note is clipped to the money. "My briefcase is my private property."

The child bangs his bottle on a chair, "Mamma, music, mamma, music." He points to the bookcase.

The palm frond leans there, curved, as if it is lazily swaying. A breeze from the overhead fan blows the frayed tips. Did she leave it out last night? Was a tip of it showing?

She is embarrassed, she never asked what he carried, nor did she let him know that she peeked. She gives the frond to the child who waves it around the house, touching the dog's tail, the backs of chairs, the dish towels.

In the afternoon, at the beach, she buries their son's legs in the sand and practices explanations in her head.

After dinner he is still not home. The child falls asleep on his stomach, legs tucked under, diapered bottom in the air.

The air is hot and she opens the windows, hoping and praying the bed won't be empty for long.

In the morning, the stereo is empty.

The next four mornings are the same.

On the fifth morning—he has never been away this long—she gathers all the notes. While the boy is sleeping, and after she studies him for signs of his father, she spreads the notes on the table in the order received. There are forty-nine notes, ranging from *Good morning, sleepyhead,* to *A little extra just because.* None of them are stern, unhappy, or challenging.

On the eighth morning, she removes money from her savings to buy cat food and a new set of bed sheets with a wild purple iris print.

On the seventeenth morning, she looks in the phone book for private detectives.

On the thirty-second morning, she stays in bed and calls her mother to babysit.

On the thirty-seventh morning, her mother says that if a person is so sick they can't get out of bed for five days, they should go to the doctor. Her mother leaves.

On the fifty-ninth morning, again she thinks she sees him in the park, but it isn't him.

On the seventy-third evening, while dancing with her son to a recording of Russian lullabies, the door opens and a man with a briefcase enters. This man has a beard, is gaunt, and pale. He says, "My name is Richard."

TINFOILERS

I

It is late afternoon and Jordan is twelve when the three white unmarked pickups drive up in the dust. Cornbread, the dog, barks and growls. Jordan calls the dog off and ties him to the trailer hitch. Men in sunglasses, flashing papers and envelopes, argue with Jordan's father.

When they leave, Jordan's father goes into their trailer and comes out with a glass. "If you ever have a bad day, this is the taste you'll want to make it better." Jordan knows to close his eyes and let his dad hold the glass. They've been doing this for years.

He isn't sure what taste to expect, perhaps lemonade, but, the flavor is cold and tremendous. Root beer, the good stuff.

They spend their last night sharing, talking around the burn barrel with their neighbor, Winnie Heald, who is also forced to move. Jordan and his dad plan to buy the property back when they make it big. Winnie says to hell with it, he's going to Oregon to work on a cousin's crab boat. The New Mexico sky is dark and wide and all Jordan's. Cornbread sleeps on a shoe.

II

When he is twenty eight, Jordan's girlfriend Pamie says that people living in trailers listen to Art Bell and wear foil under their hats to ward off governmental airwave interference.

"Tinfoiler alert." She waves to a white t-shirted man hoisting a tire toward a three legged pickup. "If he wasn't wearing that hat, the Gov would subliminally force him to donate to the Republican Party."

The man drops the tire. It bounces and rolls next to the road. Pamie watches him in the rear view mirror as they drive past. "Betcha he got that tire off Buck's Ford L250. Paid him a sixer."

"Enough." Jordan gets tired of her sometimes.

"What? Sanford and Son doesn't want his people picked on?"

"Some people live in houses, some don't."

"Some underground too. That way, the gamma rays can't reach them."

He turns up the radio. They are going to a wedding. People he has never met and she barely knows. He wants his faded Bermuda shorts and his lawn chair.

At a stop sign Jordan elbows Pamie away from the mirror to show her a fading sign in front of a closed gas station, *Freshest Chew In Town.*

Pamie grabs his hand and presses it to her cheek. "You do me right, I'll get you that sign."

At the reception, he tries to feed her a chocolate-dipped strawberry. She plucks it from his hand and shoves it into her mouth.

III

When he is thirty-three, at the early birth of his first child, Jordan calls his father from the hospital, "It's a boy. Ten of everything."

"On my way. You better let that woman of yours get some rest."

Melanie, his exhausted wife, sleeps, yet her legs still quiver.

Jordan's dad shows up with the littlest pair of fur boots and a large bag of fish and chips. He stinks up the hospital room and Melanie wakes, "Hungry."

Jordan's dad kisses the nose of the yet unnamed infant, places him in his son's lap and tells Melanie to close her eyes and open her mouth. Jordan holds the soft baby next to his neck, listening to the smallest "Ehhh, ahhh," while his father, in a soiled shirt and muddy shoes, feeds fried fish to the mother of his child.

"I can feed myself." She giggles, but Jordan's father tells her to keep her eyes closed and taste every bite.

Jordan tries hard not to fall asleep, thinking of when he was young, how he would sit under the trailer awning in the morning sometimes, mouth open and eyes closed, waiting for his father's surprise: waffles or French toast? He could usually tell by the smell.

JAMES BROWN IS ALIVE AND DOING
LAUNDRY IN SOUTH LAKE TAHOE

S tu is driving to South Lake Tahoe, to take his post-partum-strained woman to the snow, to take his nine-week-old infant through a storm, to take his neglected dog on a five hour car ride, and to take himself into his woman's good graces. And, he's hungry. Stu has considered more than once stopping the car on the whitened highway and plunging himself over a cliff, so he could plop into a cozy pile of snow and hide until his wife is logical again or the baby is able to tend to itself, but he's not dressed warmly enough for months or years in a snowbank, has no snacks in his jacket, and he must focus on The Family. The Family of four: the woman, Stu, their baby, the dog. It is almost blizzarding, the windshield-wiper fluid is frozen, the window is frosted, the dog is antsy, the baby whimpering, the woman—who should be happy, she nagged for days to go to the snow—is intermittently admiring the snow and whining about cramped legs. Stu is trapped, by the car, The Family, his own legs, and the snow, which is falling, falling, falling.

•ↄ

Megan's legs are killing her, mostly because her shoes don't fit. Her man thinks that her feet will go back to a previous size after she loses the last eleven pounds. No shoes fit and she just knows her three-hundred-dollar ski boots will be terrible. She removes her shoes—she should have done this miles ago—and feels instant relief. She is also relieved that the baby is calm. The baby coos and says "eh" and "oooh" and wiggles his little fists. The dog lies with her head on the baby's carseat. Megan remarks that this is adorable. Her man grunts.

•‿

Phillip, who is nine weeks old and does not have control of his muscles just yet, sees the dog's head and would like to touch her, especially the black circle around the dog's eye. However, Phillip's little fists go every which way, but not that way. He grunts little noises when his fists don't do what he wants them to do.

•‿

Beebop, the dog, wishes she had a yellow squeaker toy. Like the one at home. The yellow one sitting on her roundy bed. If she had the yellow squeaker toy, she would squeak it and thrust it into the fist of the baby. Perhaps the baby would throw it for her, because her man and woman never throw anything anymore.

•‿

Stu is afraid to talk because his woman might cry again. She cries a lot lately, even though he is working harder than he ever has before, is bringing in a good paycheck, and is taking The Family on their first vacation. Instead, he is silent. The snow is falling, falling, falling, and he thinks he might just have to pull over, run out into the snow and scream into the darkening forest. But, then he might get lost, and have to eat his horse, like the Donner party. But he doesn't have a horse, and the Donner party ate themselves and their horses in North Lake Tahoe, not South. They didn't have cell phones.

•‿

Megan is trying not to cry. She is sick of being fat, sick of being a milk machine, sick of not having her own income, sick of being dependent on her man, and sick of not knowing what to do when the baby cries. It is her first baby and sometimes she doesn't think she has any idea of what she is doing. She feels like an imposter and is terrified someone will catch on very soon and point at her, yell at her, and take her child away from her, because she is a crybaby. She knows this is stupid and feels even more like crying when she realizes the stupidity of her stupidity.

․ـ

Phillip watches the dog blink and this is interesting. But, a flailing fist pops up and punches Phillip in the eye and he lets out a cry.

․ـ

Beebop curls into a ball away from the crying baby who has just punched himself in the eye. The cries are a lot like the sound of her squeaker toy and Beebop lets out a world-weary sigh.

․ـ

Stu hears the dog sigh, the baby cry, and notices his woman's discomfort. He is helpless and wants to say something, but knows if he says anything, anything at all, even something he thinks is nice, or helpful, or pleasant, or cheerful, his woman might weep. And then he'd have two criers and one sigher.

․ـ

Megan squirms and through the snow reads the signs on the hotels and restaurants. The car stops at a red. In front of a laundromat, on the sidewalk, stands a dark man with black hair in a leather jacket. He wiggles thick eyebrows up and down and squints in the snow as he smokes a cigarette. Megan speaks. "Hey, look, James Brown."

․ـ

Phillip hears his mother's voice—her happy voice—and pauses.

Beebop lets her tail wag once and sits up. Mom's happy. Mom's happy.

Stu catches sight of the man. His woman is correct: there stands a guy who looks just like a happy James Brown. "He's alive and doing laundry." Stu says.

The man's eyebrows wiggle. He looks over toward The Family and opens up his jacket revealing a shirt that reads glittery, GIVING UP FOOD FOR FUNK.

Stu's woman grins. "It *is* James Brown, downtown."

The dog studies James Brown while whapping her tail on the baby's carseat.

The baby says, "Oooo oooo."

"Right on, Right on." Stu presses the button, lowering the windows. Cold pine air drifts in.

His woman lets her arm out and brings back snowflakes on her sweater to show everyone.

THE VIM AND VIGOR TWILIGHT CRUISE

> . . . no matter
> who else is shouting . . .
> you keep your eyes
> on that one place where someone like you is trying
> as hard and as long as possible not to be left
> alone, to be lost at sea.
>
> —David Wagoner, "Man Overboard "

On the last afternoon of the Vim and Vigor Twilight Cruise, many of the short-timers spend their days naked. It isn't in the rule book, or even a suggestion of the director, but rather a tradition started by a group on the first ship who thought it prudent to be bare on their final day.

Elizabeth isn't interested in nakedness; she will be modest to the end. But, her fiancée, Egbert, lounges in the sun sipping a red and white Lava Flow, straw to his pursed lips, penis slack and uninterested. Occasionally he recrosses his legs and Elizabeth watches behind her sunglasses the changing shapes of his testicle wrinkles.

"Disgusting," she says, trying to look away. "I'm no longer engaged to you."

Egbert takes the straw from his mouth and covers his penis with the tropical drink. "But, I really love you."

"You've only known me since breakfast." Now that his manhood isn't so present, she finds herself again interested in Egbert. "It was a good omelet though."

"Lets not wait until tonight." Egbert snatches a towel off the sleeping woman's legs in the next chair over and wraps his waist. "Let's get married now, so at least we have a few hours to call each other husband and wife."

Elizabeth ponders Egbert's too black chest hair and saggy-sad nipples. "Compromise. 4 P.M. starboard."

"Lovely!" Egbert lights up and orders another Lava Flow from a bouncing-by waiter.

Elizabeth adjusts her gold-beaded one-piece complete with embroidered anchors. "You're in charge of arranging it with the Captain. I want yellow tulips, a three piece string ensemble, and—" She scans the deck for ideas for outrageous demands and noticing a waiter struggling with a full tray, "a juggler."

Looking deflated, Egbert sinks back.

Elizabeth takes a sip of Egbert's drink. "I hate jugglers. I'm kidding."

"That's why I'm marrying you."

⁘

The captain rushes toward the bride and groom and then slows down as the violin player starts the music with an elegant note.

Egbert presents the ring, size six, bought in the jewelry shop on the first deck. "You don't want to make love, do you?" he whispers to Elizabeth as he slides on the ring.

"Gosh no. This is my best dress."

Egbert nods knowingly and kisses the bride.

⁘

They dance until dinner. He is not the type she would have dated before the cruise, let alone marry, too minty-fresh, too cornball-jolly. He would have been a good neighbor, or husband of a relative, the kind she could sit by at family gatherings and know she wouldn't leave annoyed.

⁘

However, he holds her with respect, not too tight, not limp. He doesn't eye the other women in the room and follows the number one ship rule: he doesn't ask why she is on the cruise.

He tells hammy jokes at the table. He gets everyone to laugh, and pats her hand several times. She is quiet. Of all the mistakes she'd made in her life, ignoring men like him is the gravest. He glances at her frequently with merriment in his eyes. She moves closer toward him and he puts a warm arm around her shoulders. "It's been a good marriage, hasn't it?"

⸜

When the sun lounges long in the sky, not quite dusk, people gather on the top deck. The music is playing while Egbert and Elizabeth dance their way toward a line that forms along the rail. "Why are you here? Is it illness?" Elizabeth whispers.

"Shhh," Egbert whispers in her ear.

The jumping takes a long time, there are at least two hundred people, all with a variety of endings. Some are drunk, some cry, some shout, some sprint, a few are dragged by the kindly crew. Elizabeth and Egbert slow dance through it all.

Elizabeth keeps her eyes closed until Egbert swipes her tear with his thumb like a father to a small child, "Goodbye, my beautiful wife." He holds her hand in his and brings it to his temple, smiles gently, then walks the plank. He shouts to the crowd, "For my final act!" takes four quick steps, balloons off the plank into a clumsy fat man somersault, and then he's gone. She doesn't even hear the splash.

Then it is her turn.

Her legs shake and tears flow. Sobs. She gasps and pants.

The captain holds her arm firmly and helps her up the ladder to the plank.

She grasps the ring with her other hand, turning it over a time or two as she walks swiftly toward the ocean, not wanting to be too far apart from Egbert's final act. He might be only a wave or two away.

ARLO'S BIG HEAD

While Arlo's parents argued, he levitated. Seven months old, ready to put the world in his mouth, and eager to jingle everything, he focused in on Dad's voice, then Mom's, while floating his head a few inches above the mattress.

"Besides, I can't hear what you're saying," his dad fiddled with a fork, "so keep it to the confines of your intellect."

Arlo raised both arms to go along with his floating head.

His mother snapped a towel on the table. "That way you can act as if I didn't say it."

Arlo lifted his legs above the crib. If he could just raise his bottom, float above the mobile—seven kinds of fluffy trains—over the kitchen, and out onto the porch. There, he could sit in the middle of his empire: his Exersaucer, where he'd be surrounded by blinking, twinkling, moving doo-dads.

"Maybe you didn't," Arlo's dad was saying while cleaning his glasses. "Maybe in the plane of existence I'm in, you didn't say it."

"I did say it," his mom thundered, "and, I don't regret it."

Arlo's head hovered above the mattress, tugged at the rest of his body, and finally led his ascent above the mobile.

His mom's voice lowered, "We're on the same plane, you dunce."

Arlo floated quietly behind his mother's back. The back porch door opened for him.

"If there are many planes of consciousness and they interpenetrate themselves," his father spoke slowly, "how can you be so sure we're here together?"

It was almost twilight. Bats swooped down on mosquitoes. One tiki torch remained lit. A moth struggled in a melting banana daiquiri.

Arlo's head led him to the kingdom of his Exersaucer. He eased his legs into the seat, reached for the green squeezie, *honk honk.*

Arlo's dad pushed back a chair. "You left him out there with the June bugs?"

"I brought him inside and put him in his crib. I know I did."

Honk. It was all better. The orange donut swerved, the yellow floppy made a *beepity-beep* sound, the red button said, "Three! Triangle!"

But then, hands reached under Arlo's arms and he felt himself being lifted. "Sorry son, we'd rather argue than put you to bed."

Arlo let his forehead be kissed by his mother, his cheeks caressed by his father. He let a blanket tuck around him and closed his eyes while his parents admired his soft skin and tiny toes. "Goo," Arlo responded, and let his body go heavy, all of it except one finger which remained pointed as if he still had something to add to the conversation, but had fallen asleep mid-thought.

THE FLOOD OF '09

few, the type who own rubber boots and full body rain gear, like Lawrence and John, stay. Hell, it's the ten year flood zone. Ever since the '86 flood, they've known the bursting river would raise unlocked garage doors and set floatables free. Refrigerators tip, career, and dump possessions. Anything wood floats.

Gary is dead across the street in the hearse with foggy windows and a busted transmission. John notices that Lawrence has been looking at it daily from their bedroom window. Even though the hearse is on slightly higher ground, there's no way for a tow truck to get through. The River Road closed over a week ago.

The neighbor rents to men from the city who come to Guerneville to pass. John only met Gary once, just after the last man died. Gary was too ill to speak and full of tubes. But John noticed a glint in Gary's eye, a sort of honor and fight. The same look John looks for in Lawrence as Lawrence gets sicker.

John moved their cars up the hill in time just before their driveway went under. The Drake Road intersection is deeper than one thinks, and every flood, taillights disappear in the murk. Living on a slight rise in the road makes the difference from having to gut sheetrock or just spraying and airing out a garage. They know how much flood-mud stinks in the weeks after.

To get Lawrence out of the house and away from the sight of Gary's hearse, John takes them canoeing around the neighborhood. They find cats stranded in water-surrounded trees, opossums clinging to chimneys, bugs gathered on everything that floats. John makes sure Lawrence stays dry. To stretch their legs, they climb out and walk onto a roof.

It's tempting to scavenge wandering Adirondack chairs. Lawrence films a piano rushing under the bridge, half submerged and tilted as if played by the invisible mad Mozart. John thinks how he will watch that film by himself some day and remember this moment. Downed trees in great clumps tumble in the deafening surge of the river. Carports drift away. Picnic tables, bottles by the hundreds, plastic pieces in every color, life vests, paddles, all the accoutrements of river living, speed toward the sea.

It's rained since Christmas. That, after an unusually wet November. The sky is dark and angry, like an unforgiving God. Attached below the bridge, the black snake of a broken power line bobs atop crests.

It is dusk. John launches rotting wood from old planter boxes off the deck into the wet gloom. This isn't their first flood, but it is the only time in twenty-six years living a block from the Russian that the shadowy water has risen enough to lap at the base of the house's piers, inching upward by the hour. Soon, Gary will be drenched too.

Lawrence says, "Poor Gary," while a floating oak limb adheres itself to the hearse's windshield wipers. Soon a white paint bucket wedges itself. More twigs, branches, and a half inflated, pink child's inner tube collectively make a barge bridging the almost submerged hearse to a redwood tree. "It just seems so disrespectful."

Lawrence adjusts his yellow rain hat so droplets don't ride down his neck. In the cold, he is sweating. "We could let him out, let him float."

"Seems better than drowning." John starts to wade across.

"I wasn't serious."

Siding and soggy cardboard push away easily. When John reaches for the car door, he loses balance, splashing sideways. Cold wetness oozes over the rims of his hip boots.

Lawrence calls from behind. "I'm not laughing."

John scans the darkening sky. "Anyone watching?" Three jabs with a solid oak branch and the wide window breaks. "It has to look like he swam out on his own."

Lawrence is shivering. "Hurry, it's his last trip."

It is easy to get Gary out of the window; he floats out, small and twig-like, emaciated, wearing a soggy velour jumpsuit. "I'm going to take him out to the current."

Lawrence teases. "I'm making raspberry pie and a roast tonight. A garden salad with fresh beets."

John eases the body past a broken carport. Knowing there isn't much in the cabinets left, he says, "I thought I said I wanted lamb, something simple." He points to where the garden used to be, "I'll go diving for parsley and onion."

John can see that Lawrence is leaning weakly against their awning under the constant pelt from the heavens. While holding the dead man's foot on his shoulder, John half drags, half swims past the disappearing eves of the river-front homes, past the riparian tips of bay trees, toward the boisterous current. Gary's body swings sideways joining the flow, like he wants to get on with it.

Even though John doesn't want to swim back home by himself, he lets go so Gary can proudly join a log covered in salamanders, a rectangle of white Styrofoam and a grubby beach ball, bouncing and bubbling all on their way toward the mouth where they'll roar into the ocean, smashing with the waves against rocks

CRUMPLE

It was ridiculous, the back pain, the platinum white flash, the bent at a two-o'clock position, the grunting, the shuffling, the I'm-only-forty-one moaning. Just a Kleenex box I picked up. Only a squirrel I was trying to wave away from the bird feeder when the spine twitched again causing me to collapse on one knee, land on the baby's bouncy chair and slap my head on the toy basket.

An hour later they found me unconscious in a crumple. Donna, who stopped by to co-dog-walk, heard the baby screaming and opened the door. The same neighbor, an anti-kid woman—one who grimaced at runny noses—picked up the baby and held him until the ambulance arrived, until my husband showed up, grease-stained and wide-eyed.

Even though I was out cold, I could hear everything. It was a paramedic who suggested holding the baby to my breast. My husband told everyone to look away while he pulled apart my robe. The taller paramedic said, "This isn't that weird, it's not like she's dead." The short one said, "Shut the hell up, buffoon."

The baby instantly quieted so everyone could think.

I woke up and saw only the squirrel who hung upside down from the birdfeeder and chattered.

THE HARDEST WORKERS

The men who labor harder than anyone else don't say hello. Instead, they have a singular greeting, "Why ain't ya workin?" Ain't no 'g' in workin'. Instead of saying, *piss off,* they defend themselves. *I was sharpenin a saw, grindin' my blade, gassin' my truck. I'm headin' out. Just gettin' in.*

They take days off only for pain: migraines, sinus, injury. They scoff. They tolerate extreme measures of aching and when they do collapse it is because the human body must fail at some point. It is fallible, unlike their work ethic.

The hardest workers sweat chainsaw oil and fuel. Everlasting black rims the tips of their fingers. Knuckles bulge and fingers angle. *Don't remember which one broke when.* Scars are dirt-lined. Shirts dotted with battery acid holes are handed down from father to son. Boots are the premier purchase and coveted when new. All hats bear the perspiration line.

Some chew and spit toward that brown dripping coffee cup no one peers into.

When they rest, they sleep on the unwashed pillow, the rolled out army sleeping bag, the sagging single, against the oak, under the crane truck, by the brush pile, near the logs, away from the D7, but not too far from the egg sandwich they forgot to eat but will on the way home.

That rock in the boot waits till quittin' time. Dented tin hats pose on top of wet wool socks and soaked boots. Hot white feet ease into romeos for the ride home.

They blow wood chips from their nose and spit grease. They wipe splinters from the corners of their eyes. They peel bark from their forehead and find tree stumps in their socks. From their underwear pours sawdust.

On the way home they stay awake by talking about who has the biggest big toe.

It is the end of the day when the body drags itself to bed. It does not itch. Poison oak affects only the weak.

SWEET VENUS

Rueben, since he is on acid and can do things like that, brings Venus right out of the painting that hangs in the bathroom at the organic café. Venus steps out and steps back in, several times, her gaze focused on the sink, her small poof of a belly unmoving. Just her left leg moves out and back.

He wants her to stride out of the portrait completely, to join him naked at a table where they'd drink hot smooth almond tea with soy milk while admiring each other's nakedness, openly, before the inevitable kiss. But she is hesitant.

Venus obviously wants to relinquish her captivity, but perhaps it is the knocking on the door (*come on, dude, I need to go*), that inhibits her. He whispers to her flat ear, "It's okay, Venus, my sweet. I'll rescue you."

But the pounding continues (*man, open up*) and her left leg steps out and in, sometimes very lengthy, that leg; it almost touches the floor, four feet below the painting. Rueben speaks softly to her, "We'll swim unclothed in Lake Tahoe. I'll make it warm for you." (*banging*)

Rueben can no longer ignore the thumping as it becomes liquid and with each bash a juicy tomato forms which pushes itself through the key hole and lands on the floor with a splat. "Just wait," he whispers, not to frighten Venus. "Just wait. She's coming." He uses a new technique; his whispered words penetrate the wood, but become shouts on the other side of the door. Why hadn't he known how to do that before? The acid opened up abilities he'd never thought of; he'd take this one with him. He'd keep it. How handy.

The banging grows loud enough through the tomato door to cause echoing. Even the paint echoes. The tomatoes, now joined with celery stalks, push themselves, squeeze themselves, through the tiny hole in the door knob, piling on the floor up to Rueben's knees. He pushes them away, wading to the door, pressing his thumb on the keyhole to stop the flow. The drumbeat of the carrots, which point their way through like bullets against his flesh, begin to infiltrate his fingers, then his hand, then his arm.

He is helpless to fight the onslaught of organic produce and falls back against the wall where he realizes flawless Venus will soon be smeared. They could drown in the mass together, which is beginning to rot. Slimy spinach caresses his neck, he slashes at his body, pulling out tendrils of green onion. He shoves away the prod of cabbage.

Using each lengthy fiber in his arm, he tugs at her frame. With a *crrrrrrp* sound, the confining border releases from the yellow wall and as his body turns, he passes by a window.

The window! How did he forget? The soupy window edges won't allow her cage, so in haste, as watermelons erupt through the sink, he removes sweet Venus from her incarceration and rolls her like a poster. "I'm sorry, V. Just for a few moments." She squirms, but he holds tightly and crawls out the window, falling onto a crate which digs pointily into his kidney. He does not care. They're free.

He runs jacketless though the November snow, down to the lake. "Almost there. Almost there." The cold traces his bare arms and then lifts off, springing away from his invincible body. Venus cries out now and then, but he insists she be kept rolled in for her own safety. When they reach the beach, he slips and bounces back up, then jumps ten feet over a mound of plowed snow using his new extraordinary capabilities.

The snow sparkles individually, greeting them, and he reaches down to hug as many as he can of his brethren flakes. They respond in kind and he smears them on his face, feeling the delightful chill in his skin as the snow reunites with his cells. "We are all one," the flakes say in unison, in unspoken words, but Rueben hears them and agrees with great joy that he is finally aware of the fusion of all cellular matter.

Knowing Venus won't want to miss the experience, he buries her in snow just briefly because of her nakedness. The idea grabs hold of his cerebellum and he feels a tug of responsibility. He removes her from the harmony of the enveloping snow, covers her delicately with his shirt and continues bare chested to the lake.

At the shoreline, he knows he should remove his shoes in case they weigh him down, but he feels the yearning of his shoelaces to swim. How unfair it would be to leave them alone on the beach, unable to splash in the forty degree water.

He unrolls a grateful Venus who gasps for air. While asking for forgiveness, he strokes her level hair. Wide-eyed, no longer staring at the sink, Venus instead indicates toward the thin early frost auditioning itself on the shore, hoping to become legitimate ice. She forgives him and shimmers, eager to lie on top of the water, letting her hair swell like a nimbus of magnificent seaweed. He kisses her fixed mouth. She responds with eagerness, but wants to swim first.

He bounds into the water, trailing Venus next to him like a rectangle kite; her feet bounce on the broken ice and flutter along. Soon, he lies on his back and floats, his bride-to-be next to him. "I never thought I'd get married."

She responds with a girlish giggle, the laugh of a girl who is just figuring out how to make her man happy.

The cold travels through his arms and lower back, but he holds Venus's hand tighter and uses his powers to evade the chill until he's fantastic, warmed by a nonexistent sun, even though his teeth rattle and his skin pimples. "I love this," he murmurs and she replies clearly, "I love you."

His eyes follow the pattern of an elaborate constellation; Venus would know its name, but he thinks he'll ask her later; he does not want to alter their enchantment with speech. He clings to a softened Venus, parts of her have torn away, but a clump remains in his hand: her hand, warm and forgiving.

They float, Venus and Rueben, past trembling, past jaw-chattering, past immobility. The contentment of their unification spreads throughout the waves until the lake buoys them with congratulations.

INTERMITTENTLY I HIKE THE CLIFF

Next to the turquoise of the cove, on the whitened beach, a sea of gray catches my eye. At first, I think it might be bobbing kelp, but not on sand. The mass of movement contrasts with pink balloons and a bonfire. Below me, a party of elderlies dance around a hunched woman who sits on a log, swaying with the music. While clutching her sweater away from her throat, her shoulders shudder. She can't breathe well. She closes her eyes and often smiles.

They dance jerkily, some with canes, others with walkers, a few in wheelchair, all are bent and aged. Their singing drifts to me on the wind now and then, but mostly I hear the buzz of kazoos and the honk of horns. I watch from the cliff edge, jealous—I'd never had a party in my honor and it is my own birthday. I cling to a bouquet of wild forget-me-nots hot in my hand. I'd picked them as a present to myself. My dog tugs at my side.

The music quiets and the woman lets go of her sweater. She stands slowly and walks with help. Two crones on each side guide her through the crowd. The elderlies chant and throw rose petals. What joy in these aged faces!

Just as my envy peaks—I'm teary with self-pity—my flowers, fine and nimble, drop to the ground scattering, when the gray-hairs heave-ho, tossing the wrinkled smiling woman into the fire.

The crashing of waves drown out the cheering. I back away from the cliff, scrabbling as I lose my balance. My dog prods me with a damp nose to rise, but my legs and arms are jumbled. I can't remember which moves how. At last I manage to stand, and let the dog pull me down the path toward my car.

At first I drive over the speed limit, passing cars, ignoring lights. But, as I close in on my neighborhood, I think of the sliver of soap in the shower and the pile of newspapers next to my chair.

I stop to purchase two items. In the quiet of my kitchen, I eat the single vanilla cupcake and toot loudly my new horn.

YOU ARE THE RAISIN, I AM THE LOAF

At 4:22 A.M., she crawls over the soft baby and onto her warm husband's chest.

"Am I snoring too loud?" He rests weak hands on her lower back.

"You snore big then he snores little. Back and forth."

He rubs his beard in her hair.

She tucks her knees along his sides. "Am I squishing you?"

"No. You're a raisin."

She reaches over to also hold a smooth baby foot. "Then you can't feel me. I'm so small."

"Too tiny. Why are we awake?"

"Thoughts. Busy raisin thoughts."

"You should try being the loaf. The loaf never stops thinking."

The river murmurs.

She hears deeper breathing again and speaks before he can fully fall asleep. "Are you sure I'm the raisin and not the loaf?"

"I am the loaf. The oaf is the loaf."

This must be his apology for earlier. She lets more of her weight ease onto his chest.

A few drops of rain drum on the awning. The few beats grow to many, drowning out the river.

"I don't need to worry about the big things?"

His breathing is even.

HANKERING

S tephen Jones, M.D. inspected Michaela's scar, while she in return inspected his name tag for the possibility of swallowing it. As the orderlies wheeled her gurney from one room to another, she spied purple latex gloves on a counter and zipped them into her mouth, chewing lightly, just enough to squish them into a wad. Dr. Jones caught this too late, and with the help of Annalisa Gonzales, R.N., wrestled with Michaela's jaw.

Michaela smiled and opened wide. "All gone."

The doctor frowned. "She's headed to surgery anyway." He added loudly to Michaela, "This is the last time we can go in through your stomach, Michaela. Do you understand? Laundry detergent, cigarettes, batteries. They can kill you."

"Anesthesia?" Michaela nodded. "Right on."

⌣

Michaela's brother Enzo tugged at his mother's earring before they entered the recovery room. "Ma, when are you going to learn?"

"I forget." She pulled out the other earring, asked the nurse for a safe place to put her purse and looked over to her son, "She was doing so well."

"They lie, remember?" He watched the swinging doors for his sister. "Part of the deal."

⌣

Nurse Gonzales wheeled Michaela into a corner, away from equipment, hanging posters, thumbtacks, drawers. "She's done. Fine. Groggy. You know the routine."

"Honey?" Ma leaned over and smoothed Michaela's hair.

Michaela's eyes fluttered. "Last time."

Enzo stood back against the wall. "Sure it is."

Without opening her eyes, Michaela spoke in a slur. "Doctor Stephen Jones says last surgery."

Ma stood up stiff, speaking to the nurse, to Enzo, to a doctor, to anyone, "What happens next time she swallows a toothbrush or a spoon and they can't retrieve it through her esophagus?"

Dr. Jones glanced up from the chart, "Too much scar tissue."

Ma pulled at her collar and pinched her son's sweater sleeve toward her.

Enzo shrugged her off, folded his arms and pushed harder against the wall. "Then what? Dirt passes the old fashioned way, but hard items? What about crayons, wire, staplers?"

They all knew the answer and no one responded. Not even the doctor.

"What about the light bulbs?"

"I really didn't like the light bulbs," Michaela murmured.

"Oh good, sweetie." Ma smiled at everyone.

"That's such terrific news."

"I'm so tired of this," Michaela whispered.

"Good sign," said Dr. Jones as he looked into Michaela's eyes with a small pen light and repeated toward Michaela's mother. "Good sign she's getting tired of it."

Ma hugged her son's folded arm. "Maybe this is it. Maybe she's done." She squeezed while Enzo flexed his muscle. "Thank you, Doctor."

She scanned his white jacket. "Sorry, what was your name?"

The doctor glanced down at his chest then sharply at Michaela who lay still like a closed-eyed Mona Lisa with just the slightest smile on her face.

AFTER MEANDERING MENDACIOUSLY
DOWNSTREAM

He fell asleep there, but woke up here. At least that is what he says, without explanation, with the bewilderment of a man who is feigning confusion, and doing a poor job of it.

Annie rolls her eyes, without even hiding her annoyance. Men can be so pitiable sometimes, a topic Janice, Barb and Annie talked about last night in front of the fire, hours before Phillipe and his dreadlocks materialized, uninvited.

Janice points out that the battered red kayak is more out of water than in, a phenomenon that wouldn't occur unless he pulled it onto the beach.

Annie is irritated by Phillipe's obvious lies, enough to want to argue, but it is Barb who says, "You mean in the middle of the night, your kayak up and floated downriver, with you in it, and without navigation, landed at our campsite?"

Annie, like the rest of the women, is the type who doesn't need Phillipe's apology nor his confession, interrupts. "What do you want, Phillipe? Food, sex, water?"

Phillipe looks toward Janice, not Annie. Janice is the most feminine of the group with her long red hair and dangly jewelry. "Ladies. How distrustful women are today. I would think three lovely ladies camping alone would be happy to see a man, just in case they needed help."

As soon as he finishes his sentence, Janice put her hands on her hips, "Phillipe. If we wanted a man around, we would have brought one."

It was Annie that came out of her tent that morning and found sleeping Phillipe and his Coors cans at the edge of their quiet beach. "I think you did fall asleep, I mean pass out, but after you crashed our campsite. With that mystery solved, now we deal with why you're here."

"And how to get rid of you," adds Janice.

Phillipe *tsks*. "Man-haters. I wake up on a beach full of man-haters."

Barb walks closer to his kayak. "Not going to have much fun without your paddle, ladies' man."

Phillipe tugs at his packs and tosses cans. "What! Where's that paddle?"

Annie points to the far shore, "Looks like it fell asleep here and woke up over there."

"Oh no," Phillipe points to the short calm space just a few feet above riffles. "I'll have to jut across quick to get that paddle or I'll be heading downriver."

Annie takes charge. There is no way a man is going to ruin their women's weekend. It took four months to plan this trip, hundreds of emails, one ex-husband restraining order and three reschedules. "Get in. We'll push you out. You can use my paddle, but better bring it back."

Barb elbows her. "Annie. He'll never make it back with it; he probably won't get to his paddle in the first place, the rapid starts right away."

Annie winks. "Big strong man. He'll make it."

Phillipe climbs in and they push.

Annie makes to hand him the paddle, but at the last instant, holds it close to herself. Phillipe heads right into the rapids, yelling.

Janice says, "Useless."

Annie says, "Prime example why I'm no longer married."

Barb mutters, "Nobody drinks Coors anymore."

It is Janice who jingles her bracelets and grabs the first drum. Barb shakes her rattle and Annie retrieves her new drum. They make music until breakfast, just like they planned.

ALL MY DROWNINGS

I'll die first. I pick singing in the shower. I will sing Bono, every song I know with my mouth open as wide as a train tunnel until my lungs fill up. I will not swallow. I will inhale the water until it pours from my mouth to the bottom of the tub where it will mingle with the regular shower water, glide down the drain and never be seen again. Like me, once I'm buried.

Edson, are you still out there? You die second.

I'm here, leaning against the door.

But, you can't pick drowning. You either get falling or choking.

I'd prefer falling, much more fun on the way down. Nothing fun about choking.

If the shower doesn't work, I'll inhale talcum powder. I'll puff the powder into a cloud and charge like a bull toward a cape, breathing in the gust of white until the silica takes over.

I hear that silica causes cancer and then you'd die a painful ugly death, not a quick romantic one.

Since you're going to fall, I think you should be chased off the edge of a roof, or chased across the top of a train.

Or into a tar pit.

I get the tar pit. That's a drowning for sure. Either way, just before you fall, the chaser should just touch your flapping wool sweater, soaked in sweat.

I've run a long time.

I'll play in a fountain, *yippee, yippee,* until my foot gets caught in a drain and I sink underneath. No one will hear me tumble and protest. The fountain will be loud and filled with playful French speaking families. Someone will eventually find my body.

It will take weeks to identify your swollen remains. You have no scars.

You on the other hand, Edson, should make a scene before you go. Commit a full-size crime. Steal something worth millions. You haven't stolen anything since several games ago.

Or, maybe I'll protest a public concern by attaching bombs to my chest.

Yes, make a name for yourself and they'll be looking for you. You'll either die a saint or a criminal. Up to you. Do you want to spread relief or pity?

Wait, bombs have nothing to do with falling. We're playing this on my terms. You get the next game.

Don't mess this one up. Are you going to be in there all night?

Let me show you my first drowning. I put weights in my shoes and I'll jump into the lake.

That's falling.

I'm not stealing your thunder. I'm jumping. Don't bodies eventually float to the top?

I'm next.

If you're going to fall from a high dive into a barren swimming pool, leave a note. Something about how you tried so hard but couldn't do it. Make them feel sorry for you. Mention people you barely know, people from seventh grade, a neighbor who moved away. Thank someone obscure—the cashier at Chevron who picked up your dropped quarter. That meant a lot to you, how he went out of his way to bend, pinch and hand back. Say *if only* the entire world picked up dropped things, you could have stayed on this planet long enough to enjoy clean floors. But, loose change upsets you so. End the note with an incomplete sentence. As if you wrote it and couldn't finish it anymore because you had to—

You need to drown sexy. Remember the spray-painted dead babe in Goldfinger? You could drown your pores in massage oil.

I will set up back to back massage appointments for forty-eight hours. I will have been rubbed and caressed so many times, my muscles will be tenderized and turn to liquid. I'll melt into an aromatherapeutic puddle. No need to burn incense at my wake, I'll smell so good.

I could die from falling in love.

Not possible. And so overdone. So blasé, the whole broken-hearted bullshit. *Bah.*

I want to go with a bing bang bong. A big to-do.

I could drown in snow. An avalanche! They'd furiously dig. The sniff dogs would paw at my ice cave. I'd yelp and say I'm getting colder, I can't feel my feet, tell Aunt Flossie I always loved her. I'd say I can't hang on. I'd cough and sputter. They'd finally find a gloved hand, but it would be too late.

I'll get to experience the leap, the mid-air flight.

Even though you get the audible, *"Ayyyyyyyy"* as you tumble in the air, I'm going to win this. Listen to how I splash in the tub. It is with the gusto of a winner.

You could submerge yourself in a vat of beer during a Milwaukee brewery tour; you'd be the straggler who gets lost. Just thinking out loud here.

On the way down, you might as well fall from on high and get a great view. Skydiving. Especially if you just tell your mate you're running to 7-11 for smokes and a donut. Be right back. Next thing you're on the news as a big splat.

If I'm going to do the skydiving feature, I think I should drop a toaster or something outlandish above someone's house. Later, they'll be cleaning their gutters and say hey how did this get here?

On the other hand, maybe drowning is just too ugly—the unsightliness of my bloated greenish body, like a stepped-on frog. Maybe I should slam my car into a wall or off a cliff, into the ocean.

There you go, drowning again.

You have more opportunities to fall than I do to drown. I'm beginning to regret my choice. Still, I'm going to win. You'll see.

You could get a job in spring as a dog groomer and inhale wads of Border collie hair. Nevermind. Sigh.

Don't even tell me you're tired of this. If you quit first, I'm number one. Don't make it so easy. Get out there and jump, you quitter.

Let's see. A hairdryer dropped in a bathtub. Splash. Zoing. Saw it on Columbo.

That's electrocution. A dip in the sewer pond. I could fall in it too. We'd be sporting flowered swimsuits and an umbrella.

A neighbor, who wished us well, would report. "I thought they were going to the beach. They looked so happy."

It is getting late. I've got to get the perfect drowning in tonight before we call it a day. I guess the prize would be life, eh?

Life.

Your life isn't worth mine, that's for sure. I come up with better ideas. I'm more creative. You're a follower. I should live, you should get canned. Plenty of people to follow around in hell. Or heaven, if you have something up your sleeve.

While we're on the subject of sleeves, couldn't you drown in silk? I don't know how you'd accomplish that, but it sounds rousing. You could sing Bono and still leave a good long suicide note.

You shouldn't have said the suicide word. Takes the steam out of our game, doesn't it? Let's just not refer to it at all and we won't have that problem.

We could do it together.

I could be lazily lollygagging amidst the lilly pads, floating on my back, and here you come, falling from a 747. You careen onto my peaceful body, send the frogs and the pads flying up in the air, splashing for blocks, spraying all the water from the pond, except that which I drown in. Maybe keep a frog or two there to croak after our last breaths.

Or is it toads that croak? I think it's bedtime.

I can't believe you're turning in, leaving me here in the tub. I win, I win.

Hand me the back scrubber and the loofah. I have business to attend to. Light two candles. No three. Fetch me a notepad. I want you to go to the kitchen and cook up something with crab. When it is done, call for me. Tell me it's ready. Tell me how good it tastes and threaten that if I don't hurry up you'll eat it all. You'll get no answer, so eat it all.

I'll eat it all and I won't wipe my lips with a napkin.

You could take out the garbage—the crab shells and garlic bread-crusts—and trip on the back step, falling onto a sprinkler head, which would puncture your eye and sever some sort of life threatening brain segment which would end it right there.

At least my belly would be full.

Crumbs would linger on your lips. Your fingers would shine from olive oil. Your pants would have stains where you wiped your hands.

They'd find me in a day or two.

Or I would.

Goodnight.

Go to bed, you loser. Let me languish in my superiority. Let me come up with new competitions. Let me lie in the tub by myself, soaking my calluses and over-worked calves. Let me lounge.

Get some rest.

Let me rest. Let me rest for good—for the love of God.

Water?

No. No, thank you, I'm not thirsty.

A GLOWING PREGNANT WOMAN

Slumping at the kitchen table with her shorts unbuttoned and the fan several inches from her face, she muttered. "I'm not built for this kind of thing anymore." She picked at the cottage cheese and iced tea, the only two things palatable these days, and inched her chair sideways, away from the view of the bed. She tossed her robe over the answering machine, to cover the blinking light full of cheerful congratulation messages from church members.

Her husband would be home soon, eager to see her, tired from work, and no doubt full of new baby names he thought of during the day. She had no dinner to present, no projects completed, nothing to show for her day, again, and yet he'd be in a good mood, as always.

The bed lay unmade as she'd slunk back in it three times today. The dishes of half-tried beans and untouched tuna attracted ants in the kitchen. The floor hadn't been cleaned in a week. The dogs flopped slovenly on the deck, given up on human attention. Books, all earmarked in the first-trimester queasiness sections, lay strewn about the house. One now appeared within her sight, on the kitchen table. She pushed away her bowl until it hit the book and flopped off the table.

She belched and supported her aching head with her arm. The fatigue behind her eyes—impossible as all she seemed to do was sleep—urged her back to the pillow.

Her bladder announced itself as it had been doing lately every hour, when the drone of the garage door indicated the arrival of the father of the blossoming fetus.

She leapt for the bathroom, steadying herself on the sink, pony-tailed her silver hair, washed her face, brushed her teeth and reappeared in what she hoped was glowing. She rinsed her mouth over and over to rid herself of the now toxic-tasting toothpaste.

"Where are my one and two?" came from the front door.

"In here." She put on more deodorant to cover remnants from sweaty naps, carefully so the Speed Stick didn't get near her nose; everything smelled wrong these days. "One sec." The mirror displayed newly forming acne and bloodshot eyes. She washed her face again and then decided he deserved better than that. She took off her clothes and started one head of the many-fauceted shower.

"Can I join you? Or are you too big for me to fit?" His after work smell and garlic breath would nauseate her, but how long could she avoid him?

"I don't even show yet." She looked out the bathroom door and let one full breast peek out.

"You're showing something all right."

She braced herself for the pending onslaught to her senses as he ran his hands down her sides, unknotted his tie, removed his shoes and clothes, and stood naked. Her pre-pregnancy brain acknowledged his muscles and flat stomach, but still, despite every intention, she scrambled for the toilet and heaved white cottage cheese into the bowl, leaving her bewildered, naked husband shrinking, as he covered his manhood and eased out the door.

FROM BOOTLEG TO BLACKOUT—
THE HISTORY OF RELAPSE IN AMERICA

I

I will never drink again, he says and asks the waiter to make the dish without wine.

II

Haven't seen him in twelve days. The dog should be rescued. A drinking man, a man who sprawled last time in the dirt with ants on his face, might not feed it. "The dog is dead," he says and hangs up.

I call from the driveway, "Send out the dog, I'll take him in the meantime."

"I'm in Willits, working," he says, "two hours away."

I say, "That's nice, you're in Willits, but could you send out the dog anyway?"

"I'm in Willits!"

"Open the door, send out the dog!" The door opens and the dog bounds into my car.

III

If my eyes were closed I would have thought I was pumping gas instead of smelling his neck. Syrup breath. He pulls down the sheet he just pulled up. Soaking pillow. Body stain. Bloated belly twice what it was ten days ago. He wipes tears and denies them.

Bewildered, like a man who got off at the right bus stop but the buildings have changed. Negative bank accounts, all four of them. He says, "I needed the money to buy cheese at Circle K." He quivers while reaching for the remote.

"The cable was shut off," I tell him, "nothing to watch."

He turns over toward the smeared window. Swirled greasy hair faces me, "I was craving cheese."

AT THE FOOT OF THE MOUNTAIN,
THE INEXORABLE

Annletta is waiting for her babies to come. Every morning she drinks tea, fills the birdfeeders so the cats have someone to watch, adds wood to the fire, and hikes the mountain with her dog. She is thirty-eight weeks pregnant—nine and one-half months.

Her belly is larger than she ever imagined it could be and harder than the firmest mattress. Still, each dawn, just after the horizon lightens, she hikes the hour to the top of the mountain, says good morning to the meadows from the peak, and heads on down, picking up small pieces of firewood along the way. She is clumsier and slower now, but careful.

The babies kick and squabble when she returns to rest by the fire. The cabin is on the north side of the mountain, and a fire is needed all day. She can feel the babies fighting as they do every morning. But, then, just as she smoothes her belly with oil, she feels them calm, snuggle and hug—then tussle again. Often in the evening, when she collapses in bed, early—it is hard to carry twins—they push and prod for a few moments, then sleep. But in the mornings, they always battle.

The crib is ready. The tiny blankets folded. Annletta doesn't believe in doctors and will have the babies at home. She is ready. Everything makes her tired. The two boys don't have a lot of room in there and she doesn't blame them for getting edgy, but their wrangling makes her tired. The thirty-five pound weight gain makes her tired. Her dog, who doesn't understand there are two babies on the way that take up most of Annletta's energy, makes her tired. The boys poke, push, squirm, swim.

As the days move closer to week thirty-nine—babies usually arrive between thirty-seven and forty weeks—she has read this in her home-birthing book—Annletta's ankles swell up as large as her calves. Her heart beats hard and loud after she eats. When she lifts her foot up on the table to draw back a sock, she notices a red line traveling up her ankle toward her knee.

A red circle surrounds a white circle. Something has bit her. While the twins poke each other, *move over, move over,* she watches the red line creep past razor stubble—it is hard to bend to shave her legs.

The line reaches her knee by nine o'clock, and by ten is heading up her thigh. The dog has pushed the squeaker toy into Annletta's hand sixty seven times and fetched it sixty six. Annletta puts the toy behind her back and tells the dog to lie down. *Night-night.*

The tip of the red line is mid-thigh. Annletta presses on it, to see if the line will change direction, head on back to its origin. But instead, the line proceeds slowly and silently around her finger and toward the top of her leg.

One of the boys hiccups a steady rhythm, causing a tuft of her sweater to rise and fall. Annletta has no insurance—why have insurance when you don't believe in medical intervention? She believes in meant-to-be's, just like the wood-cutting man she met on the mountain who made her babies.

Instead, Annletta prepares for the line to continue its march upward. But, what will the line do when it meets her sons?

She thinks she could be sad—they may die—but only if it is intended to happen. She should not stop poison, because obviously it was sent to her for a reason.

She watches the fire and the scarlet line which reaches the crease of her thigh. She covers herself with a blanket.

The babies know it is evening and they embrace. One intertwines his ankle across his brother's. After one finds his thumb and the other nestles closer, they fall asleep.

Annletta feels them sleeping and says good night. The dog lays her head on the hot skin of Annletta's lap and closes her eyes.

Annletta nods off herself, but wakes just in time to see the silver edge of sun on the horizon. Orange embers glow in the hearth.

She skips her tea for the first time ever, the babies don't wrestle, the dog whines at the door, and Annletta pulls the blanket up tight over her heart.

FOR SWEAT OF LIMBS

Our sister, the traveler, brings back a bottle of snake oil from Thailand bearing a shoddy label that reads, FOR SWEAT OF LIMBS. This happens the same month we find in a Chinese cookie a fortune that says, LOVERS ON TRIANGLE, NOT IN SQUARE. It came with the bill, a scribble of choppy Chinese, a personal affront to our brother, the accountant.

The snake oil has a cobra in it. Not unlike the worm in the tequila, but the cobra stands about five inches tall and wavers when the bottle jiggles. Our brother, the accountant, doesn't believe it's genuine. Our sister, the traveler, insists it is. "Here," she calls to him, "take a swig."

We are in a brew pub in Calistoga, waiting outside to surprise our mother for her seventieth birthday. We're on our second round. Now that everyone is here, someone should go in to get her, as she waits at a table alone, her blotchy purse on her lap, thinking she is meeting our brother, the accountant, who always has his particulars straight unless he doesn't, which is when he is drinking, full of himself and has all the opinions of Men Who Know Everything.

Our sister, the traveler, is annoyed with the accountant. He always pooh-poohs her adventures—why go anywhere outside the U.S. where parasites, jail-jumpers and the uneducated masses lie in squalor. She gets up in a well-traveled huff to go get Mom. The rest of us dip bread into olive oil and consider the lunch menu. The accountant takes off his tie, mumbling about grammatically clumsy fortune cookies.

Mom is delighted, surprised and teary eyed. Our other brother, the one-time-almost astronaut, who lives well on some sort of mysterious governmental disability, the details of which not even the accountant can weasel out of him, gives a toast ending it by lifting up the snake oil, "To Mom, to Thailand, to the glorious English language." He reads the back of the bottle, "Intentionally daub generous on skin rubble."

"God love translators," says the accountant, and even though it is October, he removes his jacket.

"Quit touching my skin rubble," the traveler says, ordering French wine even though we're sitting in the heart of Napa County.

The one-time-almost astronaut orders the French wine. The rest of us order the French wine, knowing the accountant will order a beer. As will mom, just so he won't be alone. Finally we say to hell with individual glasses, and order a bottle.

The waiter arrives, eyes the snake oil, and takes our orders. Our other sister, the former waitress-turned-belly-dancer-turned-yoga instructor-thinking-about-turning-massage-therapist, comments on the waiter's reach over Mom's head. She always comments on the incompetence of restaurant staff. She was a waitress one summer in a Cape Cod chowder house and now knows all about fine dining.

The snake oil stands in the middle of the table like a centerpiece. Someone adds a vine around it, someone adds a ring of croutons, someone circles the bottle with pepper. Our showpiece attracts the waiter's attention who adds his own contribution, five cherry tomatoes. The accountant adjusts them when the waiter is out of sight and says, "People might think we're worshipping a false idol."

This causes an argument between the traveler and the accountant. As is typical of every family gathering, the going is rough, something funny happens, the funniness gets taken too seriously, the rough get going. The traveling sister travels right on out of the restaurant. The accountant is pale, sheepish, yet alcoholically righteous. The one-time-almost-astronaut orders a bottle of Bordeaux. The former waitress-turned-belly-dancer suggests that we send out good vibes, and while we're at it send blessings to the people in Thailand who can't afford French wine.

The waiter asks if we'd like anything else, looking uncomfortable. He nods his head toward two tables away while saying that there is a man who would like to buy our lunch in trade for the snake oil. This sends us into a fit of laughter until the man stands up and walks toward our table. Oval stains descend from his armpits despite the cool weather. Except for the accountant, who is loudly sucking on ice cubes, the rest of us are wearing sweaters. The man's hair looks wet; he swipes his forehead with his hand and wipes it on his pants, leaving a darkened mark. We are instantly quiet, uncomfortable and wishing our sister, the traveler, was here to handle this.

Instead, the one-time-astronaut stands up and leads the man away from our table before he can even get close to us. They talk over by the fountain. We speculate, half amused, half puzzled.

Soon, our brother returns, places an envelope on the table, says, "I'll take this," and delivers the snake oil to the man, who leaves. The accountant opens the envelope, counts bills, and tosses it to the middle of the table. "There are forty one-hundred dollar bills here!" And then, for once, he is silent.

The rest of us reorganize the snake oil shrine now around the bulging envelope and order dessert wine, reflecting on what sort of ailment the oil must cure. Someone calls our sister, the traveler, on a cell phone; she is just in the parking lot pacing, she says she'll be right back in to find out why we're so keyed up, but if she hears one more word from our intolerant brother, she'll leave in a hot second.

Our brother, the one-time astronaut, swirls his Bordeaux and tips his glass toward the stuffed envelope. He lets the waiter know we might just stay until dinner.

Our brother, the accountant, is scratching his arm so ferociously we all look in his direction and notice the perspiration dripping from his forehead. It cascades down his cheeks and spots the white tablecloth. Although it isn't warm out whatsoever. It isn't warm at all.

THE RELIABILITY OF HORMONES

Ellen stabs Ken's good hand with her blueberry pancake-stained fork. It leaves four prong marks, a dab of cream cheese, and colors: purple for the berries, red for the blood, white for the shocked skin around stab wounds, and brown from the syrup.

If he says one more thing, she'll stab his forearm.

He says to the woman across the booth, his cousin, his skinny cousin, "Ellen's just upset from hormones. It's a rough life, trapping your man by getting pregnant."

The cousin laughs, but Ellen doesn't laugh. Instead, she stabs and stabs and stabs. They love their baby, planned for the baby, shop for the baby, whisper to the baby and are genuinely happy about the baby, until in public. Then Ken always plays machismo.

Ken wraps his bloody hand in a napkin and says cheerily, "She's got me now. Knocked up. I can't go anywhere."

As if it was her idea. As if she planned this. As if he had nothing to do with it. Ellen gulps her hot chocolate.

Ken eats his own omelet peacefully and winks at the cousin. "Guess she'll need someone to help raise the child while I'm out hunting for months at a time. That baby will be too small to carry elk meat."

His cousin keeps chuckling.

Ellen wants to stab her too. Stab her plastered bright smile. Stab her trim little arms, stab her dainty little unpregnant waist. Instead, Ellen sucks ice cubes from her water glass and spits them at the cousin one at a time.

The skinny cousin smiles, "You two must be so excited."

The waitress stops by. "Anything else?"

Ken grins, motioning toward Ellen's belly, "She's eaten enough, don't you think?"

And then, Ellen's plate flies up, out of her hands and over to her husband's face. It smashes, leaving blueberries across his head. Syrup seeps down his cheek.

The cousin beams brightly, "Catch you guys later. Congratulations again!" She scoots her trim little purse along the counter as she eases her trim little self out of the booth. Ellen watches her give Ken a quick kiss on the cheek.

The waitress pats Ellen's hand. "Honey. When I was pregnant, I cried over lost socks."

Ken spits blood and his two front teeth into the remains of his hash browns. "Gosh darn it, Ellen, muth you be so emotional?"

Ellen looks from the kind waitress to her messy husband. "Could you leave us alone for a second?"

"Sure, hon. Just let me know what you need." The waitress walks away.

Ken dabs his chin and put his arm around Ellen. "You know I'm just teasin' ya'."

Ellen reluctantly snuggles into her husband's hold.

"How is our little fellow?" Ken pats Ellen's belly and holds up a glass of orange juice to her lips.

Letting him hold the glass, she sips and sips and sips.

SISTERS

The younger sends a pic of the NaPali coast from the cata-maran: blue lapping water, lush green cliffs, pink sky.

The older sends back a blurry photo of her own foot. It is a dark photo, toes splayed, linoleum beneath, highchair leg in the corner.

The younger calls about swimming with manta rays at night, at-tracted by flashlights. One hundred thirty seven have been docu-mented and if you find a new one, you get to name it.

The older one says, "I'll call you right back and sends texts of her own name one hundred thirty seven times."

"How did you do that?" asks the younger, as she sips her third.

"Why did I do that?" asks the older. Let us ask why.

HAVING TRIED EVERY ANGLE
TO GET HER CHILD TO SLEEP,
SHE GIVES UP & SCRUBS THE SHOWER

Her shoulders ache nicely from scrubbing. More Ajax, more circles, more *rub, rub, rub*. A workout finally! She yells, "Make noises so I can hear you."

In the living room, the naked toddler grunts while bending his Wasabi, the name given to the green man at the end of the wire that pedals his feet when pushed around. Wasabi is mangled into a semi-circle and unable to cruise the living room.

"Are you reading?" Her son is grunting and must be reading the book about the pigs. She feels like a pig. Never gets to the gym. Skips walks to nap. Her mamma-gut jiggles.

The child rips shreds of paper towel and blows pieces into the air like Mom does with feathers from pillows.

"Do you see the whale picture? Blowing his spout?" She is a whale. Why didn't she hire someone long ago to watch him so she could get more rest and exercise?

He stands on his tiny wicker rocking chair and waits for the inevitable, "No standees. Get off that chair!"

"You love rocking in your chair, don't you?" She smiles while getting the muck behind the toilet, the Q-tips, the toilet paper.

He eats the corner of Suess's scary, pale green pants book, but doesn't hear, "Books are for reading."

He finds a pencil under the table and puts it in his mouth. The forbidden dog bed is a comfy place to rest and chew on a pencil. He hears mom say, "Talk to me. I want to make sure you aren't in trouble," and replies "Ah! Ffft. Fffft. Dadda." He puts a foot on the dog's

57

shoulder, a message to tell her that she can get in the dog bed with him; there is plenty of room.

The dog doesn't trust the naked boy's kicking feet and darts away.

"Are you playing with your puppy? She loves you."

From now on, she decides, she will hand scrub all the tile floors. This way she will keep some muscles in her arms, muscles that are wasting away from being a full-time single mom who never gets to the gym. "What are you doing now?"

"Mmmmmmmm." The pencil gets soft and then hard as he puts his teeth in. It's a nifty feeling to crunch on a pencil. "Mmmm."

"Do you see a cow?" If only she could go for a long walk again. If only she could just leave him for an hour or two. "Was that your cow noise?" She sees women all the time who don't have a toddling shadow. Women who can stand alone now and then.

The dog notes that the boy is resting and not prodding. She finds room in the dog bed and stretches next to his warm body.

The toddler rests a bare foot on the dog's back, who flinches but since the foot is fairly weightless, doesn't get up and move.

He hears the word cow. "Mmmmmmm." The pencil isn't all that tasty, in fact it is grainy and worse than the next-day-rice mom sometimes tries to sneak on the high chair, but so far hasn't been able to convince him to eat.

He hands over the pencil to the dog and grabs his new blue shoe instead. It makes for a good pillow and he rests his ear inside the shoe listening to the muffled *whhhshh whhhhsh whhhhsh* sounds from wherever Mom is.

She rinses the brush, reclips her hair and follows the trail of removed diaper, torn paper towels, tipped rocking chair, strewn books, and the bitten pencil to the dog bed.

In it, her sleeping son, curled like a feral child in a wolf den.

FOUNDLING

E ven after the officer arrived, the mystery child remained mum. The woman who found the soggy-diapered toddler lingered on the scene as if she somehow retained rights to the child.

The officer attempted his weak Spanish, *"Buenas días. Como esta usted?"* He tried to keep irritation from his voice.

The little one grinned, handed him the garden hose and pointed to the spigot.

"That's all I could get out of him too," the woman with the big purse said. "Guess he likes water."

The officer turned away. "I'll call in someone who speaks Spanish." He turned on the water pressure at its lowest and the child giggled while hosing down the already wet sidewalk.

"I knocked, yelled. I tried both houses on each side. Maybe this isn't even his house." The woman repeated for the third time. "He's just lucky *it was me* that found him wandering the street, not a perv."

"We've got your statement. That's all we need." He hoped she'd leave, taking her big purse and big sunglasses. He needed coffee and had forgotten his own sunglasses.

The boy, or at least the officer assumed it was a boy with short dark hair, sat down on the wet sidewalk and kicked his little feet in a puddle while grinning toward the two adults. Mud trickled down the bottom of his left foot. The officer suppressed a smile. The child was actually kind of charming the way his uncoordinated feet splashed the water and the way the droplets delighted him.

"He's certainly not upset about being without his mother." The woman dug in her purse. "I wish I had something here I could use as a diaper. That bloated thing must weigh ten pounds."

He was thinking that he wouldn't be surprised if the woman found a diaper and a box of wipes in that huge purse when he glanced again at the mud on the child's foot. He squatted down just in time for the boy to point the trickling hose at a uniformed leg and soak it. "Thanks guy. Let me see that foot."

The boy held up both bare feet and rolled backward into the grass. He laughed and kicked his feet in the air while the officer tried to hold the one foot still. He couldn't help but smile this time, the child was actually sort of endearing. "That's not dirt." There were words on that boy's foot, not in pen, but a tattoo. *Jorge Mancho, 818 Sparrow Court.* He called in the address on the radio and said, "Jorge. That your name?"

"That's my address." The woman dropped her purse. "I've never seen him in my life. I was just driving by on the way to pick up my mail. I'm not even sure why I took this road. Yes, I do, tree work. I was rerouted to this street. Less traffic."

"Guess we better go to your house." The officer decided that without the purse, the woman looked less bossy. She was also very pretty, he noticed. Especially when she put her sunglasses atop her head, holding back her wavy hair.

"Jorge?" She cocked her head.

"Mamma?" The boy reached out a little hand.

She took the one little hand and then the other. "Oh yes. Jorge."

A pang of protection leaped in the officer's chest. "Do you know this boy?" He looked toward the woman's car and noted a carseat in the back. "What's going on here?"

"Could you go grab a diaper for me, Officer?" she asked while picking up her child.

Mouth open, he walked to the car, looking back several times at the hugging mother and child, noting how she stroked her son's hair behind his ear, noting how the boy stuffed a chubby hand down her shirt. It was a beautiful sight. A sight he wanted to be a part of. A green-frog diaper bag sat next to the car seat. He brought the bag back and handed it to her.

"Thanks, hon." She kissed his cheek. "Daddy is so good to us, isn't he?"

He wiped his cheek and stepped back. He loved her kiss.

"Oh, and I brought your sunglasses."

A good memory is an excellent trait in a woman, he thought.

A cruiser slowed down and another officer waved. "Hey, Mancho. Ya'll going to the barbeque this weekend? The wife wants to see Jorge."

"Jorge," the officer whispered and then he heard himself say, "*Sí, we'll be there*," as he reached over to pat the little boy's head, his son's head, and wink at his lovely wife.

THE MANY CANYONS IN UTAH

She waits a full week at the campsite for the bruises to heal. His body is but a leaning tree at the bottom of the canyon.

Feet dangling far above, she chews salami right from the sausage itself. She bites into the cheddar too. In fact, his body looks more and more like a V-shaped bush than a man, the more she looks at it.

They aren't due back for a month. Plenty of time to invent explanations.

Anyway, he would have insisted on cutting the salami with a knife, even if it made marks on the top of the cooler.

PAPAYA, MORE THAN PAPAYA

The Mind Expansion Farm was founded by the seven of us, carried on by the six of us after H's blood-letting-wrist suicide, and after the disappearance of C, the remaining five. A week later, D followed H, and all that was left was us four, bewildered and finger-pointing. E's controlling attitude caused all the tension. No! S's lackadaisical nature let W run with things. S left, backpack stuffed in an uncharacteristic stand of opinion, promising to write from the bus station, leaving E—sweating and surly: he loved S—and W who chewed on a blade of grass while his eyes wouldn't leave the fire. And me.

I held the rest of the cultivated peyote, and in my head, the techniques for speed-growth and nutrient-boost. Quiet W had always been the guinea-pig, and E the back-to-the-beginning-idea man.

The three of us didn't like each other much by now and decided to do a sweat to cleanse our hard feelings by sending our negative vibes out into the cosmos to dissipate and return as productive ions. It was W's idea to sweat in the dark without the prayer candle. He snubbed out the glow even before my shirt soaked.

After an hour or so, E cleared his throat a lot, something I hadn't noticed when the lodge was lit. W broke the silence and offered him a piece of papaya, "to ease the swallow." It sounded refreshing. I accepted one also pressed first against my forearm until I fumbled in the dark and caught the fruit before it tumbled to the dust. I placed the papaya on my tongue; it immediately *woosh-wooshed* my taste buds, soon tri-tingled my scalp and lizard-longed my neck; right before my shoulder blades caressed themselves, a thought registered in my consciousness that the papaya was more than papaya. Whatever it was W dunked it with was trickling down inside my ankles and pooling within my middle toe.

E stopped coughing.

I wanted to ask what W added to the fruit and where he got it—he never left the farm except to ride his bike—shirtless and in dirty cut-offs, his beard and trademark outback hat. But, my tongue didn't feel like conversation, so I didn't push it.

Instead, I dove into my kneecaps, slid deep alongside each muscle, healed that old carpal tunnel injury and turned off my bladder. Whatever it was W slipped us, it was tremendous stuff.

W pulled lightly on my elbow. I realized the person humming the National Anthem was me, so I shut down my vocal cords and followed his tug as he led me out of the lodge under the blue night, the sprinkly-spark stars.

"That was good, eh?" W rubbed his beard on the back of my hand, a motion I found both scratchy-new and gruesome.

"Where's our big E?" I said while reaching wide for the Milky Way.

W turned away from me, put on E's cowboy boots and shuffled along the rocks toward his bike. "He went the way of the others." W pedaled, crunching pebbles with half-flat tires. "Here I go too." He skimmed across the grassy area toward the cactus crops and out of sight behind a dark area, leaving me and my lean-to shelved with jars of peyote buttons.

I waited for the cough of E, the return of W or even S, but heard only a very distant moo-call, or was it my beat skipping? I listened in and counted sounds in my family of veins. *La lum rush. Mer la lum rush.* It was a nice beat to tap to, and I found the lids of two jars sufficed as pretty good, second rate bongos.

LATE AT NIGHT, CLEVER MEN APPEAR
IN YOUR LIVING ROOM

Very tired, after a long drive, which fortunately didn't include highway clogging, but did include one AM station melding into another, causing quite a case of radio rage, you step into your living room, fumble for the light-switch and find four philosophers waiting in the dark.

Not feeling very philosophical, or even witty, you remain silent. Exhausted from the evening's events—including an argument with the Dim Sum restaurant manager after you complained about the thin waiter removing plates before you finished—you face the philosophers who study you with their extra deep, probing eyes, and ponder what to say.

Luckily for you, because to be caught un-thoughtful in the presence of great thinkers is one of the gravest conundrums, the red-plaid shirted philosopher starts the dialogue, "I would say you are late, but what is late?"

"Late for what?" The green golf-shirted, balding one adds, "Our thinking? It will go on before and after any designated time; there is no need for commitment to a frozen moment."

"Surely," Red points, "you don't insinuate the nonexistence of lateness."

Not knowing what you're late for, yet experiencing slight panic (I'm late!) you search for excuses.

The man in a yellow robe nods. "No justification necessary. Time is inconsequential."

"Perhaps to you." The man in black smiles.

Ignoring your tardiness, your explanations and your presence, the men talk quickly, ping-ponging their phrases. It is difficult to keep track of who is speaking.

"Who is to say my perception of time is yours?"

"Mine could be in an instant; yours could be in an eon."

"What is an eon?" They laugh.

Taking advantage of the laughter, you casually put away your coat, hat and umbrella as if you planned the overdue entrance. It is sometimes better to act as if your blunder is not a blunder after all. But, they pay no attention as you sit on the hearth.

The green-shirted man bounces in his seat. "How long is 'Right back?'"

"How long is 'See you later'?"

"How would you measure 'Until then?'"

"Until when?"

"That's what I mean. It's all irrelevant."

Your weary vision struggles to keep up with their conversation, so you close your eyes and speak, "Philosophers always use the word 'irrelevant.'"

You believe the red man answers, "We could use 'immaterial.'"

Someone adds, "Extraneous."

Another, "Superfluous."

You recognize the yellow man's voice. "Superfluous. I don't use that word enough."

"What is enough?" Someone pounds on the table. Your eyes flutter wide for just a moment and then you return to listening.

"Much more than insufficient."

"Enough is adequate."

"Oh no. Enough could be, 'Stop hitting me. Enough!'"

"I could hit you and we could see how long it takes until enough."

"I would join in."

"I also could assist."

"I wouldn't. I'd say, 'This is all irrelevant.'" And they laugh again, the laugh of men who know they are clever, and enjoy the spar.

You open your eyes just enough to notice an open bag of potato chips. "I assumed philosophers would eat something more ostentatious."

"Now, ostentatious is a good word."

"I prefer to eat food that is grandiose."

"Flamboyant."

"Brazen," while crunching, they murmur in agreement.

"Yes, brazen," you agree, "Philosophers should only indulge in brazen dining."

"Now he's talking."

"I knew he'd come around."

"Just a matter of time."

"What is time again?"

You groan.

"The moments before here yet after now."

"The difference between then and when."

"Speaking of dining and timing." You slump against the hearth, far more than any spine should. "The Dim Sum waiter stole my plates too early.",

"A premise then: There is a fixed, universally agreed upon moment when a waiter should remove a plate."

You shuffle to the bedroom. "Make yourselves comfortable. I must sleep." Before the door closes, you hear, "What is sleep?"

"When we hear snoring, we'll ask him."

"Let's finish the chips first."

"Are they finished if there are still crumbs?"

"There will always be crumbs, infinitesimally."

You draw the comforter over your head, but not before hearing, "Too bad he didn't leave some club soda. Analysis leaves me with thirst."

"I feel conjectural with a club soda, don't you?"

"Oh yes, much more abstract."

After fitful dreams of chasing the thin Dim Sum waiter through alleys, losing him at every turn, you wake to the smell of fried eggs and the sound of voices.

"Hunger, with meditation, can be eliminated."

"Hunger then would be an emotional response?"

In the kitchen, you find the yellow-robed philosopher buttering toast and ask him, "What are you still doing here?"

"You didn't uninvite us."

"I didn't invite you to begin with." You search the cabinet for aspirin.

"Our presence was requested."

"Not by me."

"A simple request is all that is needed."

"I'm too tired to absorb your un-explanation."

"Tired is a state of mind." The green-shirted man hands you orange juice. With the first sip, you feel alert. "See, all in your head."

The black-jacketed one raises his pinky finger. "The Dim Sum waiter was terminated from his employment."

A hot pang of guilt catches in your throat. "How do you know?"

"Collective unconscious."

"We can tap in."

"How?" Could it be true? "That's fantastic."

"Universal USB cable." They giggle.

You visualize the Chinese waiter at his empty table in his crummy apartment, too poor to buy dinner, breaking apart a fortune cookie to feed his family. "I suppose I owe him an apology."

"Or he to you."

The yellow-robed man hands over jellied toast, "He hated that job. You did him a favor."

"He's fired, he's happy, and we're here." The black-jacketed one stabs his wiggly eggs with a fork and points them at you in commandment. "Also happy."

Your anxious shoulders relax.

"Plus," the green-shirted balding man studies you over his glasses. "if we were standing on the moon, would we see waiters?"

Lifting juice, the red man toasts. "Not at first glance."

You too raise your glass. "Then, losing his job isn't my fault? I'm not guilty?"

"Guilt! Fault!" They cry in unison and mutter amongst themselves.

The yellow-robed man solemnly nods. "To discuss guilt will take more than potato chips."

Paper is thrust in your hand for a grocery list: Swedish pancakes to arouse ingenuity, baked shad with roe for on-the-spot deliberation, Pacific Rim mussels—good for the wit.

They pause for consultation. "Shouldn't we be concerned with acumen, requiring salmon cakes with lemon dill sauce?"

"Acumen? For that we need the Hungarian nut crescent."

Extra paper is necessary. The pen runs out of ink. Leaving them to debate remorse assuaging pastries, you slip out the door, noting how not a single one of them contributed to the bill.

PENILE BONE

There are reasons why I didn't contact Sherii for twenty years. For one, I thought she was dead. Years ago, at a party, one of those post-high school get togethers with clouds of greenish pot smoke and clusters of people conscious of loyalty and belonging-ness, feeling obligated to hang with old friends, yet on the verge of trying to meet new ones, I ran into Denise. She smoked quickly with brief drags, like a non-smoker who only smokes when she drinks, and pushed me on the shoulder too hard. "Did you hear about Sherii? Drove into the quarry. Drunk." Denise squinted and took in a longer draw, while keeping eye contact. "Could have been us."

Denise herself died two months later, although I didn't hear about it for five years since I was away studying acupuncture, not thinking about Denise whatsoever, but I did think about Sherii now and then, and how *it could have been us* that drove off the cliff into the quarry. We often got stoned at the quarry. There wasn't a rail, nor even a sign. Sure, a foggy night, anyone could have done it.

I meant to get the details from Denise next time I came home, but then Denise died drunk-driving too, only she was beheaded as she 'sailed under a semi.' That's what Dad said in that stern don't-let-it-happen-to-you voice, as if I'd taken driving into semis under consideration. The other reason I didn't try to contact Sherii, as if I really needed another excuse, because, after all, I was basing my actions on the premise of her death, was the ten bucks I stole from her gym locker in seventh grade.

She didn't accuse me then. I stared back (while sweat rolled down between thighs) into her searching and tearful eyes and denied, "I didn't see anybody" even though I was the only one in the room while Sherii showered. We stayed friends through high school, but deceit kept us from being closer. The ten-spot issue happened over twenty years prior, and I wasn't in any hurry to call attention to my crimes, even though making amends seemed to be the thing to do in your thirties, but Sherii's quarry-death made one less person needing an apology.

·♪

On the way to somewhere, during a week long visit with my parents, I saw a woman at Circle K that looked just like Sherii, but with wrinkles around the eyes and a bit of a belly. She fumbled with her wallet to buy two quarts of Colt 45. Her green uniform pulled tight along the waist and a patch on her shoulder read, DEPARTMENT OF WILDLIFE. I eased closer and read the nametag. Sherii Fonstrup. It was her and she wasn't dead.

The ten bucks didn't enter my mind yet, but those love-handles held me mesmerized. Sherii had been a varsity track girl. I believe she hurdled. Or sprinted. Something around the track really fast, I didn't recall. This version defied my imprinted vision of tall, thin, giraffe-like Sherii. She turned around, perhaps because of my critical bulge-thoughts. Guilt flushed my face as she spoke. "Court? Courtney? Is that you?" She smiled big with coffee stained teeth and I met her eyes, her large black pupils. Much larger pupils than someone should really have in a brightly lit convenience store.

"It's me. Sherii, is that you?"

"Actually it's Shur-eee now. Still spelled the same. S-H-E-R-I-I. But I gave up the Sherii lost-her-cherry bit years ago. Now the accent is on the second syllable. What do you think? Better, eh?"

I couldn't get past her shiny black pupils, so huge and offensive. I irrationally hoped the cashier might notice and put a stop to her eyes, as if their size was illegal or, at the very least, immoral.

"Shur-ee works for me. Oops, I rhymed. I like it. Sounds French. Exotic."

She swept the beer off the counter before the clerk could stuff it into a noisy plastic bag. "I'll wait for you outside."

When the clerk handed back my change, the old ten-dollar guilt flickered. I looked for reasons to stall rather than walk out the front door to stand next to bulging Shur-eee and her iniquitous black eyes. She waited exactly in front of my primer red hatchback and astonished me by taking a long swig of her beer, in public and in uniform.

"Whatcha' been up to, Courtney?"

I searched for a topic we might get past quickly so I could get in the car. "It's been twenty years. Aren't we due for a reunion?"

"Never went to any others." She put her beer into a white government pickup and stood with her hands on her broad hips and faced me squarely. "Although our first one didn't happen until year six because of Spiegel's suicide."

"I didn't get informed of our tenth."

"Maybe there wasn't one, Court. I didn't care for the longest time what happened to everyone. Now I'm a little curious."

"I didn't keep in touch with many people. Went away to college in Boston, lived in Nepal, Bangkok, and a bunch of other places. I'm an acupuncturist. Only back for the week. Just visiting my folks."

"Come with, over to work. On Saturdays, I'm the only one. I'll give you a tour and we can hang. Fifteen minutes from here." She thumbed toward the lake and I followed her hand toward black clouds and rain lines in the sky.

I don't know why I agreed to follow her. Was it her forceful thumb? The negative ions in the air?

⋅ᴖ

Gusts of wet wind pelted our windshields. We pulled into an empty parking lot. Her blurred shape ran toward a glass door and waved toward me.

We burst from the rain into an office with several desks, dwarfed by deer heads topped with extraordinary antlers. Musty rain smells and beer breath filled the room.

"I've never seen antlers that huge. Must be as wide as my car."

"Let me tell you about him." Sherii pointed. "That guy is on a quest to get laid. All he can think about is sex. If you're a female deer, look out. He'll maul you with those."

I thought she'd give me a scientific explanation. Her bluntness contradicted the authority of her uniform. "Isn't the Department of Wildlife supposed to help the animals? Preserve and all that. Wouldn't have thought they'd display deer heads."

"All rednecks in this place. Did you know that some animals have a penile bone?"

I almost laughed, but her shiny, yet flat, black eyes weren't kidding.

She shook her head vigorously. "Some get in fights and try to rip apart the other's penile bone."

I couldn't tell if she was teasing and had developed an uncanny ability to remain serious-faced, or if she truly spouted a fact I'd never heard of. "Survival of the fittest?"

She moved quickly for someone so out of shape. "Exactly. Let me show you something." We walked out of the office and through a shop where equipment lined the room. She turned a red metal circle which opened up a giant door, about six feet wide. A cloud of what I initially assumed was steam floated out. However, when we entered, I found myself in a room-size freezer. Rows of stuffed bags lined the walls. "See." A frozen blood trail, the kind that came from dragging bodies, led to a pile of animal carcasses, mostly mountain lions. Being resolved to a mostly Buddhist/vegetarian philosophy didn't prepare me for the mound of what appeared to be haphazardly strewn wild animals. A bobcat's tongue jutted as if he was biting it and blood froze on his nose in a black smear. His eyes remained large and permanently staring at my knees.

I covered my nose and mouth. "What happened to them?"

"Hunters. Trappers. Idiots. Accidents."

"Why are they here?" Blackish blood, deep wounds, and hanging entrails dishonored the beautiful animals.

"Research. Or sent to the university."

I could feel her looking at me, but I couldn't decide which was more terrible, her black eyes, or the heap of bodies. "It's a room of death. They're frozen."

"Ain't going anywhere."

She moved into my line of vision for a moment and blocked the view. I wanted her to stay right there, where I couldn't witness the awfulness behind her.

"You have to see this one." She inched behind a stack of white boxes and kicked a small fawn out of her way. *She just kicked a small fawn. It's dead, but she kicked it.* The stiff fawn slipped awkwardly across the back of a black wild pig and landed with its head in the bloody hind end of a larger deer.

I instinctively leaned to catch the fawn. "I don't need to see any more."

"Came this far. Come here, Courtney." She didn't command, but spoke as if I wouldn't defy her either. Like her simple verbal nudge would bring me closer. And without reason, I stepped forward.

Without seeing its head, I could tell by the golden fur, I was looking at deer. Its hide ended raggedly along a stomach gash about a foot long. Sherii pointed inside the gash. I leaned forward to see the curled head of a closed-eyed, unborn fawn, tucked inside its mother. "Coyote." She pronounced it 'ky-oat.' "He's over here. Hunter caught him tearing her up. Smacking away at his half-alive, tasty meal." The fluffier furred leg of the coyote stuck out from the pile straight at me, its paw aiming at my heart.

My chest shivered uncontrollably. "I've seen enough." A death smell pervaded my nostrils, which I found peculiar, as if scents should be frozen too.

She slammed the fridge shut and we warmed ourselves by the heater in the office. "That's unbelievable. Horrible. What do you do here?"

She opened her mouth, but then dashed out the door, not leaving me with much time to think, when she came right back in with her bottle of beer, not offering me any. I wouldn't have drunk anyway, since at the temple I took a vow not to put such substances in my body. She guzzled fiercely. "Never drink before four." She blinked and studied the line of liquid through the bottle. "I suppose I should have offered you some."

"I thought you were dead. Denise said you went off the Mainlen cliff into the quarry."

"I did."

"You did die? Or you did go off the cliff?" I laughed, but it came out jerky and short.

She sat behind the desk and I sat on a chair in front of it, as if I was being interviewed.

She burped. "High school sucked, didn't it?"

"I've had a lot of experiences since then. It seems like a long time ago."

"I didn't go to college." She gave me a look that flashed anger, or meanness, I couldn't decide which.

"You got a good job."

She leaned forward quickly. "Did I ask your opinion?"

No one spoke and neither of us moved. A clanking sound from back in the building stopped the silence.

"I think I should go." I put my jacket back on. "Thanks for—"

"I'm sorry. Sit. I'm just annoyed. Feeling sorry for myself." She took another swig, pulled out a pill from her top pocket, and swallowed it. "Here you are, educated, wearing a scarf, sticking needles into people, and disgusted by the locker." She peeled the label on the bottle. "Here I am, fat, used to dead bodies, and surrounded by rednecks. Where the hell is Bangkok anyway and why would you go there?" She smiled sweetly as if to make peace with me, to forget her earlier abrupt behavior.

"I studied religion along the way. Philosophy. I believe in a certain concept of destiny."

"You travel. I stay. You're successful. I mop the floor."

I didn't respond.

"I'm the damn housekeeper. I'm the lofty Environmental Service Aide. My big destiny. God wants me to vacuum. He has a fantastic plan for me to shine toilet seats." She slammed her empty beer bottle on the table, picked it up again and threw it toward a metal garbage can where it smashed. I found myself thinking that she'd get fired if her boss found the bottle in the garbage. She focused on the side wall. Her hand slowly crept to her front pocket and plucked out two pills. She chewed them slowly.

I leaned back and debated what to do. I finally settled on saying, "It seems that you're in pain, Sherii."

I expected her to leap across the desk and grab me by the throat, and I braced myself for it. But she stared at the wall for an uncomfortably long time. Finally, just when I was about to get up and quietly leave, she spoke faintly. "Why did you steal my ten bucks?"

There it was and it was all so stupid. Why hadn't I just admitted it somewhere along the way? I rushed. "I knew you knew. It was dense and I'm sorry. I'm even sorrier for lying about it."

She cleared her throat and swung her head toward me, her pupils seemed to cover her entire iris; I could not find any color. "We weren't best friends. But we were good friends. In seventh grade, you, me and Denise walked to school together almost every day."

Had we? I forgot that it was that often.

"Why, Courtney?"

"I wanted to buy lunch."

Her arms flew up in the air, reminding me of goalposts. I wanted her to bring them down and fold her hands tidily on her lap, but she dropped them slowly, leaving one hand to hover in the air, pointing at my face. "Your mom always made you lunch. I remember. Mine was wasted. She'd say, 'Tomorrow, I'll make you lunch. Go to your room. Give me peace and quiet.' Meaning, go away so I can drink."

I felt defensive but thought about what might have happened to Sherii when her mother found out she lost her week's worth of lunch money. "You're right. My mom did always make me lunch. Constantly in the same recycled paper bag. I just wanted to go through the lunch line like everybody else, instead of sitting at the table with my brown apple and yogurt waiting for all of you. Embarassing. I wanted a chocolate shake so badly."

She held a pen against the desk and pressed hard enough to dent the wood while she dragged the pen toward herself leaving a long scrape mark. "Thought you'd cop to it. I waited."

I tried not to look at the desk, but remained there amidst the weight of missed opportunities for apology, swallowing my excuses, and finally retied my scarf just to keep some activity in the room.

Her mouth quivered as if trying to settle in on the right expression. It finally established a smirk. "I don't feel so good right now, Court." She looked up at the ceiling, a little too high and too long for my taste, and tapped her foot in a rhythm. "Give me my ten bucks."

I hurried through my coat pockets and brought out my wallet while trying not to let my hands shake. Hidden behind a picture of my nephew, I found my emergency twenty and almost threw it. The twenty didn't feel like enough. "With interest."

She let the bill lie in front of her, smoothed it with an unstable hand while I moved to the door.

Her flat voice followed me. "Denise died too. Didn't she?"

Without turning around, I answered "Denise died too," and stepped out into the rain.

The heavy door, with its reflecting glass, displaying a murky reflection of myself, slammed automatically, reinforcing my abrupt isolation. "Too?" I was left to face the drenching wind as the lock clicked, keeping Sherii safe from people like me.

A STORM WATCHING SINGLES GROUP MEETS ON A CLIFF HIGH ABOVE THE MOUTH OF THE RUSSIAN RIVER

The woman at the end of the cliff shuffles diagrams and warns me of the mother ship's arrival. I thank her and watch the band set up under an awning. A man with a duct-tape covered guitar case walks from boulder to boulder sitting on each one briefly.

"Do you see the man with the bass in the rain?" The UFO woman says.

Even though it isn't raining yet and the man removes an acoustic guitar, I nod. The air is salty.

A man wearing a down vest, carrying a clipboard sits down. "You're making a scene," he tells me.

Me? I point to my chest and then at the UFO woman, "Not her?"

He adjusts his lawn chair closer to me. "She's a regular. Everyone's used to her. You and your dress, they're not used to."

"You want to know who I am." I move my chair closer to his. "Here is my Divorce Check." I set it on the clipboard. The check is white with green trim. It is unblemished. I haven't folded it yet. The corner flips up in the wind. "Never had this much before." I take the check back. "Let me introduce you to my Divorce Dress. The Papers are in the car, less than a few hours old. You guys are my first Post-Divorce Gathering."

He nods like he knew it all along. "Although this is an event for The Unattached, you want me to put up the blockade?" He puts both hands on the clipboard and looks me in the eye. "The dress says yes, the 'tude says no. I'll keep them away if you want."

I know the answer to this question, yet I ask anyway, "Are there any worth getting to know?"

He cleans his glasses. I wait. A man's opinion about another man is worth a thousand psychologists. "Only one; he'll be here soon. Around eight."

"Let me guess," I say, "he doesn't say much and he doesn't stay long."

"Mostly." He nods and points toward the darkening billows. "Storm should be here in twenty-seven minutes. My prediction."

The UFO woman has spread her diagrams on the ground using rocks to hold down the corners. She is giving an earful to a corduroy-coated man.

The leader taps a pen toward her, "Estelle, your territory."

She sighs and pulls her diagrams closer to her. I hear her say, "Three bright lights, then two short ones."

The check is signed by my ex-husband. His signature is the same as always. No indication of remorse in his M or anger in his T. The amount has a lot of zeros. I no longer own a house.

The wind is whipping the leader's dark hair away from his forehead revealing just a tinge of white roots. "Tonight, your first night. Might be too early to meet Mr. Eight O'clock."

"I should go through the twelve steps of grieving?"

"Four steps? Five?"

"I should cash the check first."

"At least."

"Live a little?"

"Some."

"Find myself?"

"You bet."

I fold the check and make a perfect crease. "Does the mother ship come every night?"

"Nah. Just once in awhile," he interrupts Estelle. "When is the last time the mothership came, Estelle?"

"Thirty-seven days ago, two hours, and thirteen minutes."

"Estelle," I say, "do I need an invite to get on board?"

She scrambles up her papers and moves her lawn chair next to mine.

The leader gives me the you-asked-for-it look.

"Eight o'clock," she says.

I look into her soft brown eyes, sane as I've ever seen. "A lot happens around here at eight o'clock." I slide the check down my dress and into my bra.

"Do you really want to go?" She searches through her purse and comes out with a well worn, frayed green toothbrush. "Here. You'll need this to get in."

It's seven fifty-seven. I hear a car pull in behind me, but I don't turn around. The leader nods to the newcomer and glances at me. I thank Estelle, put on my new Divorce Coat, and leave my lawn chair.

I walk out past the band. The man on the congas tips his head. The guitarist checks out my legs. I step out of my uncomfortable Divorce Heels, kick them off the cliff when no one is looking, and continue barefoot down Highway One.

I carry the toothbrush in my left hand. The other hand I hold to the sky where my palm is greeted by rain.

TEARS OF THE APACHE

Safe from the chill outside, three three-legged dogs, one snoring, sprawl on bean bag chairs in the corner of the shop. The owner, of the dogs and the crystal store, busies herself with sorting a shipment of aventurine while a shoplifter pockets three silver necklaces, two greeting cards, and a handful of pine incense. The shoplifter, a woman in long coat covering a blue-green batik ensemble, eyes a dreamcatcher but thinks again, the dreamcatcher's bulk would be noticed underneath her shift. Instead, she carefully balances a Tibetan bowl in the crook of her arm and slips it down the sleeve into the sewn-in bag along her underside. Carrying two books, one about tarot readings and the other of Hindu statues, she says gaily, "I think this will do," as she approaches the cash register.

The owner looks over her glasses, "Did you find everything you need?

"Lovely store." The shoplifter gazes tenderly toward a stained glass vase. There was a time she would have saved money for such an item.

"After my daughter's accident, I bought this place." The owner rings up the dreamcatcher, the incense, the bowl, the necklaces, the books, all the while the shoplifter gasps at the pending tally flashing on the cash register. "Was that two or three greeting cards you snagged?" The owner flashes white teeth, but the shoplifter thinks she saw a glint of something blue in the back of the owner's throat.

With her back toward the shoplifter, the owner places the books into the sack and turns around baring a smile this time that flashes a cold blue flame-like light. No teeth. "Sure that's all?"

Sweat runs down between the large breasts of the shoplifter. She reaches into her purse, picks through her wallet, never taking her eyes off the blue flame that quivers in the half-parted mouth of the owner. Her husband will leave her if she is arrested again. He won't even post bail. He made that very clear last time. Skipping over the seven stolen credit cards, she retrieves her own Wells Fargo debit card and drops it on the counter.

The owner smiles with eyes of aquamarine and places a hand over a polished stone hanging around her neck. "Smoky quartz. Aids in awareness and channeling." She touches an earring, "Azurite, cuts through illusion." She shakes her bracelet, "Chrysocalla, helps clear subconscious imbalances."

A yawn from one of the three-legged dogs takes the shoplifter's focus off the blue flame. "I think I have enough."

"I don't think so." The owner's cold breath chills the shoplifter's forehead. "You need obsidian, also called Apache Tears. Volcanic glass. It absorbs, disperses negative energies."

Reckless words drift from shoplifter's mouth, "I need Apache Tears."

The owner tilts sideways and rummages around under the counter. She lifts out a rock the size of her forearm. "Largest one I know of. Weighs about eighteen pounds. Used for introspection."

The shoplifter places her hands on the cool crystal tracing the rough edges with her fingers. "What do I do with it?"

"You'll know." Blue flames lap about the mouth of the owner and then disappear behind perfect teeth. "Would you like a receipt?"

The shoplifter seizes the rock to her chest and lurches out into the snow toward her car. Despite the frost on her windshield, she opens her windows and turns on the air conditioner. She holds the obsidian in her lap while snow graces the windshield. It piles up along the windshield wipers while the sky darkens and the red OPEN sign blinks out. The owner of the store locks the front door, surrounded by her dogs. She waves to the shoplifter who turns off the engine and places her lips to the icy volcanic glass.

Snow covers the windshield, the hood, the trunk. It pools around the tires, smoothes over the bumpers and fills the tracks from the shop owner's car. White blankets the shoplifter's driving arm and she thinks about crying, but can't.

THE CLOSET

The only place she could begin the story is from the closet, behind the wool winterpants and against the down jackets. This is where he would bunch the jackets in the corner, after moving the boots to one end, always wishing the door would open so he could throw something out to make room. But that was always such a silly thought, because if he could open the door, he would be out himself.

He wanted to write the story first, based on just peeking underneath the door, shoes passing by, clunking of heels perhaps? Clogs? Or were they men's shoes, cracking with concrete, or slippery from sleet. Either way, from a study under the door, he would have been an expert in the where-you've-beens of those shoes. He would memorize the sounds: the *clack, clack* I'm home, the *crunch, kick* of snow, the *tat, tat, tat* of hurry.

He didn't write the story first. She wonders if he thinks about the mouth pressed to the carpet, the face sideways to get a look out through one eye? What would be the best way to see out of the bottom of the closet door?

She had to get in that closet herself, similarly to how he did, but on her own. Not forced. she just sort of landed in it, light off, shut the door behind her, puffed around in the coats, swore at the hangers, elbowed the vacuum cleaner, bunched the down jackets just like he said. Made a comfy nest for herself and waited for her eyes to adjust, which they never really did, just noted the long stretch of wishy-washy light at the bottom, revealing the tip of one cowboy boot and the corner of a box.

She had to scramble around several times to rearrange the floor items until she found the right length of side for her body to fit. But, she forgot that he had to remember where it all went and put it back as fast as possible when the feet appeared. He was supposed to stay standing and not touch anything.

Even though he said there wasn't a light, she looked anyway. Felt above for a chain, smoothed the walls for a switch.

He never knew what time it was or how long. He couldn't tell time then.

From below, the satin insides of sport coats, their square tags. No matter how hard she strained, she couldn't see them or their color. Was it a blue sleeve she held?

While she tested the closet he asked what she wanted for lunch and she told him to hush, he shouldn't make any noises other than those he would have heard back then, so she could really experience the closet. He said, "Fine, experience it then."

There were dank smells, dust smells, shoe smells, scarf smells. She gathered pieces of floor gristle and moved them to the corner. She tasted the paint on the wall. He must have done that at least once. She scratched the back of the door and ran her fingers on the door frame.

She smelled grilled cheese sandwiches and called out that she was ready.

Clunks and sizzles in the kitchen and the sound of a chair being pulled back.

She rattled the doorknob.

The *crick, fizz* of a soda.

She yelled.

A *chink, tink* of a fork.

She kicked the door like he must have many times.

Two coughs.

She shouted, "Please."

The front screen door slammed.

Silence.

She pleaded.

No response.

The light under the door paled to nothing. She couldn't get much leverage kicking. Not enough room.

·ᴖ

84

The rattle of the doorknob.

He opened the door with the napkin in his hand and wiped his mouth. "I'm writing it."

"Yes," she whispered, "you."

Her legs walked to the table and sat her body in the solid chair while he served melted cheese sliding off sourdough bread, in the large kitchen, a kitchen large enough to fit fifty or so tightly packed bodies.

FISH FISHY

She is in the fish tank hiding from her husband.

"Get your hands out of the water!" he says.

She realizes that he can still see her even though her hands are plunged, so she dips down to the elbows.

"You'll mess with the PH balance."

She lowers herself to the shoulders. The water is cool. Bubbles float toward her from the treasure chest. The catfish taps by her fingers. The water smells like fish tank.

"I just cleaned it." He pulls aside her hair that floats along the top. "Seaweed, sweetie," he says. "You can't fit in there; this is only a twenty gallon tank."

She tastes the water on her bottom lip. Wet, slightly rank.

"Don't drink from the aquarium please."

Her eyes are submerged and marbled in the back mirror. Hair wavers past. With a dry foot she pushes off her husband's leg and is entirely in the tank. Her clothes hold her down, so she pulls them off and throws them over the edge where she can see her husband catch them and hang them by the fireplace.

He is large and blurry through the glass, holding a net.

She breaststrokes through the fern and slides beneath the shipwreck.

The catfish opens its mouth and closes it. He opens, closes. She does the same, reaching toward his whiskers. Above she can hear, "Come on, hon, come on. I apologized, didn't I?" The net swishes by.

She drifts underneath the fish, one leg wrapped around a fin, the other drifting lazily in the decorative rock.

THE ENDLESS LINE OF KNOTS

I

After a month of lying in bed, occasionally nourished by a banana popsicle, she caught sight of his plane through the bird-poo dotted skylight. She knew it was him because the plane flew directly overhead across the plastic dome from North to South. He was coming home, seated in 15G, chewing ice, running his hands through his hair, impatient to see her.

She rose out of bed, unsteady, and took a shower, ran to the corner store (literally ran, lest he called) bought cheese, crackers, wine, grapes, lit candles and wandered around tidying until three hours had passed. He should have been there in an hour and a half. At the latest. When, finally, the sky darkened and she realized she was a fool, she blew out the candles and eased back into bed. At least she had changed the sheets; they were cool and smelled good.

Another plane, this one seemingly poised for a long time above the skylight, glinted and dipped a wing. She rose—just in case the earlier plane was a sign to pay attention to *this* plane—cleaned, bathed, ate and waited. No him.

After one more plane crossed the skylight, she got up on the roof and covered the dome with a tarp. She placed rocks to hold it down in the wind. The room was now too dark, she opened the always closed blinds. She could now see from her pillow an expanse of northern sky and noted many planes traveling from North to South. Every plane carried him, every plane crashed before it landed, every plane was empty.

She closed the blinds. But still she could hear the planes. He was in each one, asking the stewardess, "How long until I get home, until I see her?"

II

Her mother came again, with bags and concern and directions. Bathe, clean the litter box, open the windows, get fresh air. Mom put the contents away and asked what she could get her. A stereo that could play CDs twenty-four hours a day so she didn't have to hear the planes. "Planes are loud," mother agreed, and returned in an hour with a seven-changer CD player and twenty-five on-sale CDs. "If you tire of these you can always play the radio. Happy now? Good because I'm going on a month-long cruise. You have money, the store is at the corner. Honey, you'll be all right, he's just a man. Plenty more in the sea."

III

She imagined herself knitting for the baby that grew in her belly. Mom still hadn't noticed; by the time she returned from the cruise, there would be a grandchild. Her stomach, round and huge, loomed above her.

On one of her rare days to the store, she bought knitting needles and yarn, and hurried back to the apartment. She would knit a baby hat, or a sweater, or a sock. She had no idea how to knit whatsoever and couldn't bear going out again, so she invented a stitch. Cross, loop, over and through. When she made many of the stitches they stretched into a line. She had no idea how to add another row, so she continued the long line until the ball ended. And then tied in another ball, another and another. Her line of knots was very long but would someday somehow fit together into a baby blanket. She bought more yarn, more cat litter, more cat food, more popsicles.

IV

He found her, in the corner, listening to CDs, greasy haired, hunched over her line of knots. "Honey?" She didn't look up. She rocked with the motion of the knots whispering. Cross, loop, over and through. "I'm here. I'm back. Can we talk?"

She continued the line, but the cat walked over to rub on his leg. At least the cat is happy to see me. He stepped closer. "When is the last time you took a bath?" Cross, loop, over, and through. He held her thin arm and lifted her. She dropped the knitting and shivered. "You need to take a shower."

She had seen him walk in thousands of times. Embrace her, forgive her, miss her, cover her with his lips. It was always in her mind. Like now. But she took a shower anyway. And when she got out, wrapped in a peach towel, smelling fresh, she stepped into her bedroom and found him still there, pushing the cat off to make the bed. She smiled; it was great when her apparitions also changed the bed sheets. While he stroked her hair, she slept.

The baby kicking woke her up. "It's coming." He told her there is no baby. "The baby is coming," she screamed. He searched her cabinets. She lay on the floor with her legs apart pushing. "It hurts. It's coming."

"Where is your medicine?"

"It's too late," she screamed, "it's coming."

Her shirt was drenched in sweat. She removed her pants and underwear and hiked up her shirt to free her huge belly. She rocked her thin bottom on the carpet.

"I cannot stay. You are a thin spread-eagled woman pretending to give birth." He left again.

"I am?" She sat up to face the open door. The smell of spring brushed in with a breeze, faint against damp temples.

THE TOPOGRAPHY OF A WAKE

To avoid her husband's casket, Virginia counts her family members and places them outside in the landscape.

Her brother Ralph, maroon-faced with bourbon, brashing opinions, is a mudslide over a main road, seeking attention by holding back cars. Messy, earthy and ridiculously unpractical.

Joking, straight-spined, her brother Hal, the mouth of a river, almost inviting for a swim, almost soothing, except for the kelp or seaweed or whatever you call that knotted green stuff on the shore, bubbly and smelly.

Sister Susan, following Hal's lead, surrounds him with amenable laughter. As a natural dam, she prevents salmon from spawning, even though it is known they might not survive.

Flitting through the kitchen in her barely clothed sinewy body, Virginia's sister-in-law Sheryle, the scrappy beginnings of a tumbleweed, bends to pick up dust no one sees.

Virginia avoids the eyes of the avoiders to watch her mother orchestrating. Mother has become those ants that evade an ant trap, meandering on the kitchen counter, mingling in the fruit bowl. Traipsing in an irrefutable line toward the sugar jar.

Outside somewhere, her father, long dead, that mountain in the distance, prominent from every angle, until an avalanche of infection sheared off the top, without giving anyone much time to run.

Her husband lies silently in the casket, as silent as he was in life, an alpine lake, one she found hiking. He was clear and unexpected, surrounded by snow-capped mountains. No one believed her that the lake existed; they didn't want to make the hike.

Virginia disintegrates the walls, the family. They fall away with the swiftness of a New Mexico lightning storm. The house is gone, revealing merely the pink sky and her husband, barely visible above the casket edge. Just his nose and one eyebrow.

She inches down a little in her chair and the nose dips behind the horizon of the black casket, leaving only Virginia, an uncharted archipelago floating birdlessly in the kelly green sea.

KALISPELL

There are nights, such as this one, this thirty degree, dark, but a full moon, where chimneys smoke, dogs bark down-river, and the stallion with his purple mane paces. He puffs and snorts, trots a bit past my window. A flash of an eye, a flish of a coat is all I catch through the finger-printed glass. I could ride him in the moonlight. I could stay here by the fire.

SHE APPEARED UNTO HIM

Waiting for the tug, the location of the next woman, he trembled on the bed with the dog at his side, her head dropping off the edge. The window exposed white, snowy sky, immoveable as if also waiting with him to graciously accept his role.

He already knew to prepare with fresh tattoos and a shaved head; the scars itched on his stomach. The new one needed some sort of bad guy; he didn't have a handle on it yet. Only a vague vision in his forehead revealed a brunette squelching out a cigarette with her heel, looking up to catch his eye as she blew smoke from her sorrowful mouth.

He dropped down for pushups until his chest collapsed on the floor and his lips pressed on the dusty carpet.

This last one wanted an aging artistic hippie, but one with a dangerous past. So he arrived as a sculptor with warrants.

One desired an unmotivated intellectual to prod; he donned glasses and carried Proust. The girl before needed a father figure; he obtained a conservative suit and developed a responsible yet nonjudgmental attitude.

The dog tilted her head, the black patch hiding one eye, and seemed to tell him, *they aren't yours to keep.* He gazed back at the dog, the dog rested her head on his arm, sighing. He tapped her nose.

He toyed with the dog's ear, while waiting for a clear message. It came foggily, in the form of the brunette, who would be turning the corner of Seventh and Melody at 4:47 P.M. She would swing her purse, and inhale the city air, fresh compared to the motel room where she just spent a lousy fifteen minutes for only eighty bucks.

She'd be smoking her cigarette while praying for the right man to come along and save her.

He nudged the sleepy dog. "It's time."

On the way, he practiced a rough face, as if life and bar fights left his lips permanently embittered.

THE SINK HOLE

Jerry Hichowski, Dee's husband, snapped his suspenders and pointed his crooked nose toward the sinkhole. "Dee, would you get a load of that."

It looked like a deep mudslide or an earthquake crevasse, but none of that made any sense; their property was as flat as a crab-grass filled parking lot, and nobody ever heard of quakes in Wisconsin.

"Holy Moly," Dee said, nudging a clump of dirt with her toe; it moved closer to the sinkhole, but it was Jerry who gave the clump a swift kick, hard enough to make it fly right in the center of the opening and disappear without sound.

"I'm thinking I just might push the old D7 Cat in there with the new John Deere."

Jerry punctuated his sentence with the snapping of suspenders again, a noise that often made Dee flinch when she didn't see it coming. Now that the boys left for college, Jerry's quirks weren't as laughable without their sons around to giggle and imitate the snapping behind his back.

They turned toward the side yard, filled with rusted tractor parts, mowing equipment and farm implements. A sore subject between Dee and Jerry. A sore subject with the neighbors too. Even though Jerry kept it all between the barn and the house in what he considered 'even rows,' Mib Laughey, across the way, in a house up a slight hill, looked down upon Jerry's rusting graveyard of unused items and often commented things like ". . . Had a wonderful Thanksgiving dinner, but sure wish it had snowed so the relatives wouldn't have had to gaze upon so much equipment during the pumpkin pie."

"You can't do that. What about the water table?" Dee loved the idea of losing the Caterpillar, the largest in Jerry's collection of I'llfix-it-laters, but it didn't feel environmentally right to just put a bulldozer in the dirt and cover it up with tulips. That is, if the tulips didn't sink as well.

"No diesel in it. Just metal." Jerry pointed over to Laughey's driveway. "Both Mib's trucks are gone. I'm going to do it right now. If the boys were here, they'd try to stop me."

"Could you blame them?"

"Nope."

"I don't know about this." That he would finally get rid of that eyesore after twenty years sounded too good to be true. Dee didn't bother continuing her protest. When Jerry decided to do something rather than just talk about it, she knew after twenty-five years of marriage not to get in his way. "I'll just go back and make breakfast."

"That way you never saw anything." Jerry chuckled as she retied her apron. "Nice figure Mrs. Hichowski."

"Why, thank you, Mr. Hichowski." She walked back to the kitchen and heard the whine of the John Deere's turbo. The smell of burning diesel wafted in. She put down the spatula to close the window and shouted out, "Be careful now," even though she knew he couldn't hear her over the roar of the dozer. Still, he looked up. They had always been like that, knowing each other's presence at odd moments. He tipped his head to her.

"You can't just bury a bulldozer," she muttered to Orson, the dog, who lay at the door flapping its tail. "You're not going out without a leash, not until we do something about that hole." She stopped to pat Orson's head. "It's no small potatoes; that thing would just swallow you up."

And with that comment, she realized that the gaping mouth in the acreage might not be as innocuous as it appeared. What if it spread while Jerry was out there playing bury-the-evidence? She turned off the oven and went out by the droning, with her hands on her ears.

Even though the noise made it impossible for him to hear her coming, Jerry turned to meet her eye as she marched across the yard. He switched off the John Deere. "Yes, Mrs. Hichowski."

"What if the weight of this contraption widens the hole and you go down too?"

"You sell the farm and move to Florida with your sister."

"I'm serious, Jerry."

He fired up the engine and wiggled his eyebrows at her, something he'd done since their high school chemistry class. She stood with her hands on her hips. Breakfast could wait. She trotted back to the kitchen and came back with the phone. Just in case she needed to call 911. Jerry saw her and winked.

The D7 rolled in unceremoniously, lay sideways, then slowly slid. Jerry never took his eyes from it, but Dee scanned the main road to watch out for Mib Other-People's-Business-Is-My-Business Laughey.

He tipped in the chicken coop. In went the hull of a jeep, a non-working refrigerator, an engine block to what car she wasn't sure, and to her private elation, the ancient washer and dryer. Quicker than she imagined, Jerry maneuvered back and forth, eliminating the yard from decades of I-might-need-this-someday and you'll-never-know-when-you-can-use-it.

Soon, half the junkyard—she only called it that when she was really mad with Jerry—had disappeared, leaving just tufts of tall grass that had grown between the items. How nice the yard would look once those tufts were mowed. Jerry pushed in old fencing and both piles of tires. A Toyota that hadn't run since 1977 followed. He pushed in barrels, rotting firewood, fence posts, air compressors, coolers, a rusty ladder and two doors. He left a small pile of dirt-bikes, deserted by their grown-up sons, but dumped in a waist-high pyramid of plastic oil containers.

"What the environmentalists would think of this." She said out loud, her voice drowning in the clamor as Jerry maneuvered sheets of tin. On the other hand, if they decided to sell, Jerry would have to take all of this to the dump; it would be in a landfill anyway. Her kitchen window would now cleanly face the red barn, not the red barn with garbage in front of it. She always loved that red barn, it was one reason they bought that place twenty-five years ago.

He paused the John Deere in front of her collection of spare flowerpots, her only real contribution to the junkyard, and shot her a questioning look. She shook her head. In summer, she could line the walkway to the barn with flowers. Now she was the one saving something; what a switch. In just a few minutes, he bladed over the tufts leaving almost an acre of rubbed dirt. "There's your garden spot," he yelled from his high seat.

He wasn't wearing ear protection, again, and Dee pointed to his ears. Smiling, he put the muffs over his head and skimmed dirt to cover the items in the now-filled hole. Soon, it looked much like a raw yard, without even a depression.

How naked the new garden area was. Hard to believe it used to be filled with jutting and clashing metal. She could plant a few rows of apple trees, some pumpkins, lots of lettuce, and—

"Anything else to go Dee?"

She shook her head.

"Your mother-in-law?" He turned off the dozer leaving startling silence and a ringing in her ears.

The yard groaned. She lifted an eyebrow toward him. "Yards don't usually groan."

"Ours does."

They walked back to the kitchen holding hands. "Two years and then Florida." He squeezed her hand, finally giving her the answer to the question she tried not to bring up too much, ever since her sister moved to Sarasota.

She squeezed back, her head filled with plans. "Who knows, I might fall in love with my garden so much, I'd never want to leave." Looking back at the yard, she noticed a cracked area had spread and opened up a few feet, aiming itself toward the house. She tugged at Jerry's arm and pointed. "Makes me kind of nervous."

"The land's going through an adjustment. Digesting." He nodded toward the crack and opened the door for her. "We'll sell this twenty. Build that cottage over by the woods. I'll punch in a driveway from the other road. We don't need a big house without the boys, just enough room for them to visit. And their someday kids."

"You think of everything."

"I'm thinking three eggs and a biscuit."

He removed his muddy boots in the outer room. It took Dee almost the first seven years of their marriage to train Jerry not to traipse dirt in the house. He set his boots in the row, next to her galoshes. Dee prepared herself for the inevitable post-boot-removal I'm-ready-for-breakfast suspender snap.

WHAT CAME AFTER SHE LEFT HIM

I

Upon receiving the eviction notice, Whit doesn't own a gun or bullets, but stands in his kitchen pointing at things and going, *Ka-boom! Ka-boom!* He opens fire—*puh-puh-puh-puh*—even though he doesn't own a gun or bullets, pounding the refrigerator, killing the cabinets, demolishing the stove. The room remains intact. Not feeling enough liberation with his trigger finger, Whit eases his now ex-girlfriend Sharon's filet knife, a gift from him on Valentine's Day, from its unused matching set and threatens the furniture.

The futon couch and end table do not shrink in fear despite his intention to kick them, so he turns toward the window, and studies his boot for the potential boot/glass damage ratio, finally declining the possibility. Whit slides open the glass door and steps out onto the deck toward a pumpkin. "Yahhhh." He chops it in half easily, without strength, as the blade is sharp—he sharpened them himself the day before Valentine's Day and several times after, sharp enough to slide through a human neck in a single blow.

The eviction notice comes in the same week as the water shut-off letter, the pink Pay Now! electric bill and the twenty-four-hour telephone disconnect card. *Calm yourself,* he says in his mind, *you're not as trapped as you think, time to go collecting.* He reaches for the phone. "This is Whit. Anytime you want to settle that bill, I'd appreciate it." "Whit here. Case you already sent that check, disregard this call. If not, please send it right away. In fact, call me. I'll pick it up." "Hi. Trying to clean up the books."

Sharon's main complaint was money. Whit's philosophy: get enough to get by and have lots of days off. So what if she paid more toward expenses. He took her places she'd never been, camping on the mouth of the Pack River, hiking along the creek. He brought her coffee in bed every morning, gave her backrubs, wrote songs for her and sung them by the rock fire pit he handmade in the back yard. He did one thing worth more than all her paychecks: he listened.

II

His notebook—which functions as an accounting ledger because for a self-employed guy, a simple notebook does the job—indicates cash due from customers totals more than he needs to break even with the landlord. He puts off the final call, making coffee first, and protects his belongings by stashing the knife in the side of a rope bag.

Nora Schwartz, real estate salesperson, one of the wealthiest people in the county, owes him the bulk of the money. The notebook indicates she owes a growing amount for five months. No wonder she is wealthy. However, since she has that way of talking—*Don't you ever wash your truck? Can you make this look as if one of those big professional companies did the job?*—as if his job, trimming and felling rotten and dangerous trees, is beneath her social status, he prefers to deal with her in writing.

Nora is also Sharon's aunt. Sharon pushed him to work for Nora, "She has lots of connections."

After sending all those invoices and reminders, still no money received. The only acknowledgement was a call right after the third bill. "It couldn't have taken four hours for what little work you did." But Whit set her straight, "Try to find someone who will work cheaper." The other calls were sweet. "Whit darling. Need a little clean up on a home on the West side, maybe two hours." All her "shouldn't take much time" calls meant a few days worth of work and detailed bills, proving every moment of work down to the most ridiculous detail. "Seventy-two branches drug to truck, thirty-seven minutes driving time to and from dump, four logs cut into firewood totaling fifty-four pieces."

He paces, practicing what to say. Punching the numbers, he hopes Nora can feel the aggression in his dial.

"Nora Schwartz."

"Can't wait any longer. I'm coming by to pick up a check."

"I'm glad you called. A tree almost fell on a Colonial. Imagine how that would have affected the sale."

He counts his dirty fingernails before speaking, a technique he learned long ago to use with the rare difficult customer. "Before I do anything else for you, Nora, I need that money. Five months worth."

She snorts. "Wrong. You've only worked for me a few times."

He stiffens. "I've sent invoices and reminders."

"Yes, I received them. They were so inaccurate. I'm sure you'll square away your books one of these days. Anyway, let me give you the address."

He feels an ugliness shift inside him, rather like the gradual slide of snow on a windshield. "Give me the address when I pick up the money."

"Whit, don't be silly, we can deal with this later. All you do is chop branches down, can't be that much."

"I'm on my way."

She laughs as if he suggested having the moon take over his accounting. "No. I'm leaving, and I won't be back until the Rotary Club dinner; everyone will be here in two hours, the cooks are preparing. We're having duck. Can you believe it?"

Ducks. Hard to believe? Whit hangs up with his thumb. That small move feels better than slashing the pumpkin.

Sharon had said she wanted to cook more. He spent a lot of time reading about knives, searching for the top of the line set. A stupid top of the line set that she left, along with three cartons of plain yogurt and the plastic bag with one grape in it.

He hoists a Husqvarna chainsaw into the pickup. The longer he drives, the more his mind turns over Nora's laugh, "All you do is chop branches."

He pulls up in front of her white pillared home. Nora's black Lexus is pulling away, Nora at the wheel, a man and another couple inside the car. She pulls aside Whit and flits her hand, a flit to dismiss him, "Another time, Whit. I'm giving them the neighborhood tour."

He holds out her detailed bill.

She speaks to the people in the car, "This neighborhood is filled with professionals. Doctors, lawyers."

As she turns away at the corner, he pulls into her driveway. With giddiness he slaps her invoice on the hood of a deep blue Rolls and holds it down with a strip of duct tape. Cooking smells waft from the kitchen.

He reaches for his door handle and then hesitates; in the midst of Nora's opulence, the handwritten yellow invoice flaps in the wind while the Rolls gleams. Yellow was Sharon's favorite color. She drove a yellow VW Bug with yellow spotted car seat covers and wore a yellow bathrobe. Blooming courage spreads throughout his being. Grinning, he removes the filet knife from underneath the seat. In less than three minutes the conical shapes of the bushes lining the driveway are reduced to whittled stubs.

After revving the chainsaw, he heads for the Italian Cypress lining the other side of the driveway. Feeling tranquility he hasn't experienced in months, he hacks off the limbs on the left side of each tree.

Sharon could never understand the joy of working outside, the liberation of his art. By God, he loves his job.

The grapefruit trees, seven in the front yard would need climbing spurs. Whit climbs the first, saws the leafy branches, leaving a skeleton. A woman steps out the side door, wearing an apron. He waves his gloved hand and she waves back, turning her frown to a smile. Whit rappels down and merrily trims three more. Each branch falls to the ground with a satisfactory swish.

While standing back to admire his work, naked trunks surrounded by strewn branches, dotted with yellow grapefruits, the Lexus pulls in. For just a moment, a pang of embarrassment flashes through his mind, until a screaming Nora leaps out of the car and bustles across the lawn in high heels, slowing down her approach to awkwardly step over branches. Whit adjusts his climbing belt.

"What are you doing? Stop it. No!"

He turns. "You were right. This didn't take any time at all."

"No! Did you hear me? I said no!" She slaps him hard.

"Wish you put that much energy into signing checks, Nora."
Whit stabs a grapefruit with the tip of the knife and holds the yellow roundness close to her pale face.

III

He introduces himself to the other guys as Cliff. They don't bother with last names. They're working the crab boat for similar reasons: job burnout, avoiding women, skipping bail, needing a change or quick cash. "Just show me what to do. I'm good with directions." He almost says, *I'm great with a knife.*

The sea is rough, but not as rough as the guys say it'll get. The sky is darkening and the wind picking up. Cliff is looking forward to rough.

SHE CAN'T HEAR YOU,
SHE'S CHEWING HER PLACENTA

The psychic predicts that Rose will go into labor while eating a ham sandwich. Rose wants to have her baby in a hospital, under direct supervision of an M.D., with an epidural, pitocin, and loads of morphine. Her older sister Holly, also pregnant, is planning the alternatives: hypnobirthing, underwater delivery, father cutting the umbilical cord.

"What about my sister, Holly? She's pregnant too."

"She'll have it in a tree." The psychic adjusts her purple headscarf while petting a miniature Dachshund.

"Sounds comfy." Rose has been visiting the Harmony Fair, where Holly works, once a week since she moved in with her sister, but only today on a whim has she been tempted to try the empty psychic tent. Usually the psychic sits at her card table alone, blowing her nose occasionally, but not restless. The Harmony Fair is supposed to be about health, but instead is about patchouli oil, hairy armpits, clouds of green pot smoke, tie-dyed rags, and maybe one booth of free massages with an empty chair that says, *back in ten minutes.*

Rose feels devilish. "Are they having a boy or girl?"

"Boy." The psychic coughs into a kleenex and inspects it. "Thirty dollars."

⌣

Rose is a dental hygienist with her first job. The minute she makes enough money to get her own apartment, she is leaving Holly and her husband, Al, their smelly feet, their moldy shower, and their pseudo-vegetarianism. They've been nice in letting her stay, but she wants her own place, with a bathroom that always has toilet paper.

Rose leaves the tent, armed with Holly and Al's secret: a boy. She stops by the whole wheat pretzel stand to say good bye to Holly, but a boy with a green Mohawk is licking cheese off a spoon behind the counter. "Did my sister leave already?"

He points the way with his Mohawk. "She's getting a henna tattoo."

Rose follows the direction of the bristles. A shirtless girl draws intricate designs on Holly's ballooning abdomen.

Rose admires the Aztec symbols on her sister's stomach. "Thanks for getting me in for free. I have to go back to work, but I wanted to first tell you I know if you're having a boy or a girl."

"We're definitely having a boy or a girl," Holly says while chewing on a pretzel.

"The mowhawk guy was licking the spoon."

•⌣

Rose is in the kitchen making a ham sandwich. A week after visiting the psychic is when she got her first craving for ham sandwiches. Al, her brother-in-law, is on the couch asleep and making sounds like *hmmzz, hmmzz, ahh*. Al spends most of his time on the couch because he is a student. Al has always been a student. Every time Rose walks in the room, Al turns off the TV and picks up a book.

The baby in Rosie's belly is turning around and around. Just as Rose cuts her oat bread diagonally, wetness spreads between her legs.

There shouldn't be wetness, yet.

She moans, "Oh no," the knife drops, her legs sink to the cat hair speckled floor, and Al appears in the doorway. "Rose?"

She is still holding a piece of mayonaised bread and places it on the floor. "I don't want to look."

"No, you don't," Al says, his face white. She follows Al's crooked buttons all the way down his stained shirt then back up to his graying beard, his greasy hair, then back down toward his dirty pants.

"My keys are in my purse on my bed."

Al scratches one gray socked foot with the bottom of the other. "Now, Al. Hospital."

He moves out of the doorway and Rose finally looks down. What she hopes is clear on her pants, is reddish.

⤴

Despite the fact that Rose was making, but not eating, a ham sandwich, Fern is born that afternoon. She is early, underweight, although healthy. When the doctor tickles her feet, Fern smiles and the doctor calls her a ham. Rose is sickened by the idea of ham even though she's eaten mostly just that since her visit to the psychic. The father is a married dental teacher (Holly calls him the MDT) who thinks patient flossing should never done by a man—*hands too big,* he says.

The MDT doesn't return her calls. Rose is okay about that—she can have Fern all to herself.

⤴

Oak is born in a tree. This is what Holly says, but doesn't give out details, just that the birth was trippy. Al takes his first shower in weeks.

⤴

When Fern is a month and a half old, Rose calls the psychic. Even though Rose is still sore, still tired, and still living with Holly—who spends most of her time in her room with Oak who never cries, and Al, who is suddenly clean and reading—she spends the money on Madame Fuscia.

"I want the perfect life for Fern. What should I do? What should I avoid?"

"Cigarettes, red meat, fast cars, more men with rings."

"How did you know?"

"I'm psychic." Madame Fuscia rolls out a handful of stones, exposing a rumpled Kleenex tucked in the wrist of her sleeve. "I see that your sister doesn't listen to you. That is okay. She is on her own path."

"You remember that I have a sister? You said she'd give birth in a tree."

"She did." The psychic picks through the stones. "She won't listen. Don't bother trying."

"Listen to what?"

"The silence of her son."

⤳

Rose takes a nap with Fern snuggled near her breast, warm breath on her armpit, and is happy. While half sleeping, she vaguely acknowledges the door opening. A swish sound awakens her and she opens her eyes to find three week old Oak at the foot of her bed. The baby is sitting up, his flat blue eyes staring past her.

Rose has a fleeting thought that Holly will blame her for taking Oak and propping him up at the foot of her bed. But, she notices that Oak isn't propped up at all, he's sitting on his own, months ahead of developmental schedule, and so she screams.

Al arrives first, hair wet from a recent bath, the third in two days. He stops short of the bed, begins to reach out to Oak, and then stops.

Holly arrives next; she hasn't showered in days and her hair hangs limply. She pushes away Al, scoops up her son. The boy continues to stare through Rose even though he's been jostled. Fern sleeps.

"That's not normal, Holly." Rose's heart thumps.

"My baby." Holly holds Oak tight and rocks him.

"Rose didn't say he wasn't your baby." Al looks at Rose and Rose looks at Al. They both look at sleeping Fern and Al points. "That's what an infant should be doing."

"He's just ahead of the timetable." Holly rushes out of the room carrying Oak, who as usual doesn't make a sound.

"I'll make her some chamomile tea," Al says.

Tea will not quite take care of this, Rose thinks to say, but instead says, "Good idea. Then call a doctor."

Al makes to leave and then comes back. "We—she doesn't believe in doctors."

"If you don't, I will."

"Right. Righto." Al tucks in his shirt, another thing he never used to do.

❦

After twelve phone calls, Rose finds a curious child psychologist willing to make a house call. They make a plan that the doctor will pretend to be an old friend of Rose's from college, just stopping by. Rose doesn't let Al in on the scheme.

When Dr. Giraf arrives, in a velvet lapelled jacket, Rose offers him some of Al's tabouli salad and shows him Fern. "Isn't she just perfect! My sister has a baby too. Holly, bring Oak in. Dr. Giraf loves babies."

Holly, who has purple circles beneath her eyes, brings out Oak wrapped in a rabbit fur. "His totem is the hare," she explains.

Dr. Giraf says, "Beautiful babies. Do they notice each other yet?"

As if on cue, Fern waves a tiny fist toward Oak and they all laugh. Oak pushes off his rabbit skin. Fighting his mother's hold, he breaks away and crawls off the couch in only his hemp diaper, toward the door. "Whoa!" Dr. Giraf says, "I thought this baby was just a month old."

"He's early," Holly says, beaming.

Rose is sickened by the beaming. Al looks like he might throw up himself.

"He's should be almost a year for that type of behavior." The doctor frowns, looking more skeptical than astonished. "But, he certainly looks young."

Rose holds Fern close to her chest, as if Oak's peculiar behavior could be infectious. "Fern's on schedule, don't you think? I mean, she's not behind the norm?"

Holly strokes the rabbit skin and talks toward Dr. Giraf, "Al, get the other half of the afterbirth out of the freezer. His birth date is on it." She moves her head to get Giraf's attention. "We're waiting to bury it on the next solstice."

Dr. Giraf won't look at Holly though, and instead asks Al, "Can I hold your son?"

This suddenly makes Rose nervous and embarrassed to have called in a perfect stranger, a velvet lapelled stranger to butt into her own sister's life. She feels a surge of protection for Oak, who is trying to reach the door handle.

"I think he wants out," Holly says. "He likes nature. He's an Aquarius. We had his chart done, and his rising sign—"

This is when Oak, on his tiptoes, reaches the doorhandle, turns the knob, and before any of the four adults can make a grab, his eleven-pound body is out the door. It shuts behind him, almost catching his tiny heel in the crack.

Holly is the first to the door, "It won't open. Oak!"

Al pushes her aside, "The door is stuck somehow."

Dr. Giraf goes to the window, "He's crawling down the street. My God, he'll be hit by a car."

The shriek of brakes scar the air; Holly runs for the back door, "Oak! Oak!"

Rose stays put on the couch with Fern who is still sleeping. She figures three adults in this mess are enough. But, curiosity gets the better of her and she delicately places Fern on her shoulder and pulls back the curtain. Sure enough, Oak is crawling down the street between the lanes. Cars pull over and a woman rushes out to pick up the baby.

"Don't you touch my baby." Holly runs into the street, but she is too late; the woman is already holding Oak, wrapping the ends of her cardigan sweater around his almost naked body. Holly and the woman argue while both tug on the child. Al tries to explain that Oak opened the door and crawled off, "He's never done that before, so we didn't know he could." The woman looks at them like they are insane; it is Dr. Giraf who calms down the scene with words Rose can't hear through the window. Soon Giraf is holding Oak, his little knees reddened from crawling on pavement. They are all coming back to the house. A police cruiser is wailing and the cardigan woman is flagging, pointing, and downright hysterical.

Fern sleeps through all of this.

Everyone gets back in. Holly locks all the doors and pulls down the shades.

Dr. Giraf keeps saying, "Remarkable."

Al keeps saying, "Holly? Holly? What are you doing?"

Oak, who is in Holly's arms, is not crying nor trying to crawl away. Instead, he is smiling, the toothless grin of a baby. But not a cute baby, Rose admits.

Rose kisses Fern over and over again and whispers to her how much she is loved and how normal she is and how, unlike her Auntie Holly, she won't let her be near any clouds of hashish, won't drop acid while breastfeeding, *will* take her to pizza parties and to drive go-carts, let her eat steak and chicken skin and all the cheese she wants.

Rose skirts along the wall while the police bang on the front door. After stopping to pick up the diaper bag next to the back door, she ducks into the laundry room. As soon as the police enter, Rose and Fern exit quietly, leaving everyone else to explain. It's the best Rose can do.

⁓

Rose takes Fern to three different doctors for a well visit. At each appointment she is assured that Fern is developmentally on schedule, healthy, and happy. On the way home from each of these, she stops for celebration's sake, to get two scoops of vanilla which she licks to the bottom in the parking lot. Her new apartment is clean and decorated minimally. She has no phone and hangs only photos of Fern. If she has to go out, she occasionally drives by the married dental teacher's house, but never Holly's and never Madame Fuscia's. Although she thinks about visiting them occasionally, she finds excuses. Like today, Fern needs some fresh air, so they stop at the park. Rose spreads out a blanket and the two of them lie down underneath a maple, face up toward the branches and the leaves, none of which are falling.

THE HOUSE TO OURSELVES

After a week of leaving leftover meatloaf and French bread, or half-eaten cereal at the edge of the back yard, I tried to bring the boys a little closer to the house. When I set down spaghetti on the back porch, the taller of the two stray boys asked for a fork, please. I yelled for my husband Robbie who came running. While grasping Robbie's arm, I pointed. "Say it again boy, say it again." But the child scampered thirty feet away or so, shoveled in the spaghetti, wiped his hand across his mouth and dropped the plate. The littler one had already run into the woods, forgetting his meal.

"A talking boy!" my husband cried while locking the door and barricading it with a chair.

"Maybe they escaped."

"Makes no sense." Robbie talked in hushed tones as if we just witnessed Santa Claus and Jesus Christ themselves walk hand in hand through our living room. "They got 'em all in the sweeps."

"Maybe not."

"You'd think we'd have heard of any still loose."

The rest of our evening was shot. Our kids were at Summer Adjustment Camp so we had the house to ourselves. Robbie couldn't get any reading done; I did half the dishes. Skipping our nightly shower, we got into bed early, whispering in the dark underneath our skylight until the moon passed overhead.

That night's conversation rarely strayed from the sightings of the two boys. "I told you not to feed them," Robbie said halfheartedly, "But now, what do we do? They've been civilized at some point. Someone taught them something. They're not completely feral."

I rolled over and rested my head on his chest, "Wonder why they haven't been located and herded in already?"

Robbie stroked my hair. "We turn them in to Protection Services, they'll euthanize them. We try to keep them, the census will track them with night infrared."

"Your parents would just flip. Your mom would have fainted." I smiled in the dark, thinking of Robbie's self-righteous mother, always making snide remarks about the superiority of purebreds, always pooh-poohing our adopted childrens' accomplishments that I loved to wave in her face.

Robbie's chest heaved as he snorted. "No kidding. I would have loved to see her expression."

We laughed for awhile and, somewhere in conversation fell asleep. In the middle of the night, I found myself awake. Robbie mumbled. I gently prodded his shoulder.

He reached back, took my arm and wrapped it across his stomach, "I miss the kids."

I didn't answer. I was thinking now nice it was to have him all to myself.

.ـ

In the morning, Robbie announced that he was going to work from home, but he wouldn't bother me if I needed to study. I spent the day pretending to read, but mostly making up excuses to walk past the windows. Finally, around two, Robbie put down his papers with a huff, "I haven't done a thing all day. I've read this report three times. Nothing is sinking in."

I was lying on the opposite couch with my book over my eyes, having given up hours ago. "Let's go look for them."

"We can't do that," he said weakly. I knew he was waiting for a semi-forceful statement to convince him to go out. He didn't want it to be his idea. And that was what I had been ruminating about for hours: his lack of standing on his own when it came to a controversial subject like this. He would back me up, but it always seemed as if I was the spearheader, the rebel, and he was the supporter.

"What if we get caught with them?"

"What if?" I sat up. "I've been thinking about this all day. What if their parents died? What if they were our kids, we died, and your mother who loves anything with papers, even if it is inbred and retarded, kicked them out? Ever think about that?"

"Mom would never—"

"Yes, she would." My book dropped to the floor. What I was saying was macabre, but perhaps true. Who knows what that spiteful woman would do? "She might not even take them to the pound." I knew I'd already made my point, knew I'd won, but I intended to capitalize on the moment, to dig the spear into his dreadful mother just another inch. "She might just leave them out to beg."

"She wouldn't." He stood and rushed toward the garage.

I sing-songed, "They'd be caged, then killed anyway. No one is adopting anymore."

After all these years, ever since we adopted, against the advice of our friends, relatives, and social experts in the media, I'd been waiting to put that last claw into Robbie about his mother. Now that his heart was filled one-hundred percent with love for his rescued children, he could never legitimately stick up for her purebred frenzy. He was weak and I was strong.

Without food, the boys most likely wouldn't come near, nor did I really think they'd be back after our reaction yesterday. We probably scared them. I moved the chair, opened the glass door, and walked out onto the deck, being dangerous, being daring, being more courageous than Robbie. But, as my eyes settled on the barren swing set he built last year, I acknowledged to myself that he was a good man and a good father. He missed the kids terribly while they were at camp. I sat on the edge of the deck and rubbed my temples. What a mean person I was, toying with a father's love.

Even though I heard noises in the kitchen, I stayed put, because I hadn't yet thought of just the right admission of guilt. It had to be sorrowful, meaningful, honest, yet I couldn't give in too much and take away the truth of what I'd said.

Before I could come up with the right phrase, I could feel Robbie behind me. He stepped onto the lawn, carrying two plates, both with forks jutting from them. "Hold these a sec." I took the plates of warmed-over spaghetti while he dragged one of the lawn chairs to the far end of the yard near the tree line. He came back for the plates and marched them over to the chair, removed a pad from his pocket, wrote something, tore off the note and eased it under one of the forks, "If they know how to use utensils, maybe they can read."

His face didn't look as if he had been crying, but looked exposed. I shrunk away, as if I'd spanked an infant. "Babe, I'm—"

"Stop." He sat next to me. "Don't say anything."

Now I felt not only as if I'd spanked an infant, but I'd also kicked one. "But—"

"No."

We waited in silence, the only sound our occasional slap of a mosquito.

Robbie finally cleared his throat, "They come back, I'll put in adoption papers immediately, we won't accept no for an answer."

That took me by surprise. I didn't want any more children. I wasn't even thinking that far ahead. I just somehow wanted the curiosity, the thrill of the forbidden: feeding wild ones. "But what about tests and studies? What if they're not compatible or diseased or . . ." I tried to make it sound like I was expressing his concern rather than my own. As if, of course, I was willing, but was playing devil's advocate on his behalf.

"Doesn't matter. We'll take them and we'll love them and we'll all adjust." His eyes flashed a reserve and a combination of coldness and heat I rarely saw in my husband. "You don't want them to die, do you?"

I couldn't even find it within me to protest against those eyes of his; I found myself not wanting the abandoned boys to die, but to stay far away, to find another home that needed them more than we did. A home that needed to provide charity, as we had. The swing set proved it. Others of the rare families that adopted hid their children in the house and whisked them away to special schools in dark-windowed SUVs. We had done enough. It wasn't that I wished the boys ill, but our lives were faultless now, with our two socially attuned adoptees and our house and our cars and Robbie's job and my classes and . . .

He was still looking at me, but I avoided returning his gaze. He was right: I should have never fed them. I only wanted a risky moment, not a permanent change to our well balanced lifestyle. Some of the more liberal neighbors were already awed by our good deed, and I had by now proved my point to his mother; no need to actually take in more beggars.

A branch moved, but it was just a blue jay investigating the noodles. I went inside, pretending to finish my book, while Robbie remained on the deck as the sun disappeared behind the forest. Finally, he opened the slider without looking at me and walked down the hallway to the shower.

When I heard the sound of water running, I ran for the spaghetti plates, dumped the food down the garbage disposal, returned the empty plates to the table outside, scrunched up the note and threw it in the grass, double-checked the locks on the glass doors and turned off the outside lights. Everything was just perfect as is. Removing my clothes, I joined my husband in the shower, making sure he wouldn't be coming out anytime soon.

BECAUSE CONDOMS SEEM SO DESPERATE, SHE ALSO BUYS A FERN

His wife and son are both giggling in their sleep. Hers is a lovely laugh, the one she uses when something is absurd, like when she came out of Longs with that plant.

The boy's is a gleeful giggle. Perhaps he's dreaming about when the dog chases him after he's stolen her ragged bone.

He tries to think of something humorous so as to join in their laughter, but all he can think of is bills.

He turns on the tiny book light, clips it to a hat and walks to the kitchen where the watercolors and paper are still out. He dips in a brush and adds to his son's splashes, green 'S's for dollar signs, red hearts for lips.

From the bed, the two laugh. The cooling night drifts through the window along with frog sounds.

He mixes yellow with brown and paints long legs, just like the one exposed beside the sheet in the bedroom, the one that got him here in the first place.

THE MATTER OF BLENDERS

Because Kelly Mae is exhausted from collecting the blenders that appeared in their back field, she fails to argue with her thirteen year-old who insisted on driving. It isn't until they reach the terrible intersection, the corner of 116th and River, when Kelly Mae looks across the stick shift and says, "I'm in the passenger seat of my own car."

"Mom," Nate responds, "you're too tired."

"I am. But I'm the only one with a license."

"I won't tell Dad."

Kelly Mae presses her forehead to the window. "I just pick them up and pick them up, but brand spanking new appliances keep appearing."

Nate drives five miles under the speed limit. "It's dark enough; I should turn on the lights?"

"A mixer mixes, a blender blends, a mother mothers, a hen hens."

"Right, Mom."

She notices that his hands are at nine and three. He leans into the wheel. He is wearing his seat belt. "How did I get so lucky to get a son like you?"

"You're the luckiest," he says, not taking his eyes off the road.

In the morning, she snuggles next the flannel shirt of her husband's sleeping back, only to find it too soft and too square and much more like a pillow. He sits on the edge of the bed, bare-butted, hands on his knees. "Watcha-doing?" She reaches across and pinches the closest cheek.

"Crap. It was my turn to watch and I fell asleep." He arches his back and his flannel shirt covers his nakedness. "Forget telling. See for yourself what arrived at around 2:16. I gave up and came to bed after that." He brushes hair from her eyes, "Just leave it all there though, at least until after breakfast."

⁓

Nate is already on the back deck taking pictures. As far as the eye can see, microwaves, all G.E., all white, stand on their ends.

"Why us?" she says to her son, who still has enthusiasm over the phenomenon, enthusiasm Kelly Mae and her husband lost weeks ago. For Kelly, it was the morning of the fondue pots.

"I called the Salvation Army to pick them up." Nate ducks a little.

"I'll deal with your father. By now, hopefully he won't care if the world knows."

"It's that you guys are so tired. Everything isn't the same anymore."

Kelly Mae puts her arm around her son. He rarely lets her do that these days, Nate being almost fourteen and not wanting to be a boy.

"Plus, Mom, the garage is full of dehumidifiers. The barn is packed with woks and bun warmers. There are people who need microwaves. People don't *need* blenders."

When did he become so logical? "Right, son."

Over corncakes Nate tries to convince his father that he will tell the Salvation Army that the microwaves were placed there as a prank by an eccentric cousin who just left town. "Dad, if we just play it like a joke," Nate's voice cracks, "you can blame it on me."

Kelly Mae agrees and tosses her glances back and forth from the kitchen window's view of standing-on-end-microwaves, which from this direction look like gravestones, her husband's worried brow and untouched food, and her son's chin, now sporting five hairs.

Her husband finally picks up his fork. "You might as well give them the toasters too."

⁓

A moving van appears. A team of volunteers sweeps through the windy grasses hoisting microwaves on their shoulders. The leader asks if Kelly Mae still has the boxes and if they're under warranty.

They want to plug each one in to test, but Nate, in his new assertive manner, says, "Hey, they're new, they're free, they have factory tape across their doors."

⁙

By 3 P.M. the field clears. Kelly thaws out a chicken and thinks someday she will only be cooking for two just like years ago before Nate was born. She walks out back, legs brushing tall grasses and delicate flowers.

Nate's dad comes home from work, nods to the field and his son. "Good work. People will appreciate those."

⁙

They eat dinner at the picnic table, in a row, facing the emptied field.

Kelly Mae follows her husband's gaze to the quiet, purpling sky. She almost says, "What do you suppose will show up next?" Instead, she draws her hand across his full belly and teases their son about his changing voice.

Nate deepens it even more, "Don't mess with me."

THE OTHER SIDE OF THE DIAPER

Our brother thinks he is too good to change diapers. We're not sure where he gets this from; even Dad admits he changed a diaper or two in his time. Our brother says he won't be able to handle the stench—plus it's women's work. He's the last in the family to have kids, we tell him that newborns' number twos look a lot like mustard and smell like wheatgrass juice. He doesn't buy it, even though it's true.

It is not until they eat real food that the diapers are pewy, we tell him. Still, he shakes his head and points to his very pregnant wife. *Her job,* he says.

We buy him a bouffant Dolly Parton-type wig from a yard sale for fifty cents. Dad inspects it, turns the wig over and over, says big hair will fit your brother's big head, and buys a wrench set.

Wrapped in pastel paper that reads, "Big Baby Boy!" the wig is placed on our brother's doorstep with a note: *Too manly for your baby's bottom? Wear this.*

He and his wife send us a picture of him in the wig. He is usually bald.

They send another picture of him wearing the wig and his wife's one-piece, flowered swimsuit. Bits of curly chest hair and tattoos peek from the straps.

A week goes by and we receive a photo of him sporting the wig and a used bridal dress from a yard sale. The dress is ill fitting. "White is not your brother's color," Dad says and frowns.

A month later, our brother's wife calls. She is concerned because she came home early and found him wearing the wig and her swimsuit again. *He tried to pawn it off as a joke, but she doesn't find it funny anymore, maybe it is her hormones,* she says, *but would we come get the wig?*

While our brother is at work and Dad stands lookout, we swipe the wig, the swimsuit, the bridal dress, and help our brother's breathless wife put a lock on her walk-in closet. *Nothing fits anyway,* she says.

Our brother calls and wants the wig back so he can play a prank by wearing it to the baby shower. We don't fall for his ploy, plus we already gave the wig to Dad, who insisted we put him in charge of it. Dad says he put the wig away with the suit and the dress, somewhere secret, somewhere safe.

THE RAIN

Say you sit on your porch alone in the rain. Say your shins get wet, then soaked. Say you left the baby in with his father. You know you could rescue the crying infant. You've done it all day. You have a breast that will calm him in seconds.

But, the rain feels very, very good.

The father is inside, frustrated, shushing, pacing. Say you hear this. Say the rain pours so hard your mismatched socks are drenched.

The baby is wailing. The father is trying. You hear, "Any suggestions?" You pretend the rain is splashing too loud on the roof to hear, too loud on the deck, too loud along the barbeque and on the baby swing left out in the elements, sure not to swing again.

Say your chest shivers. Your fists are balled under the meager blanket. The blanket sags, heavy with water on one end. The fists tighten every time the howling escalates.

The rain is dripping down your temple, down the back of your collar.

Say the sobs are smaller. The sobs dampen.

You hear the rocker clicking, the father humming.

Say you un-ball your blue fists and tiptoe in.

THE SPACE BETWEEN TWO SENTENCES

As the Mexican hands me the salsa, I can tell that he has murdered someone. That's all I know, other than he could do it again. His culpability shows in the grim way he holds his chin, as if his face never knew a smile, not as an adult anyway, but maybe as a child under five. I see him often at lunch-time and I watch, looking for murderer-type signs, but he doesn't carry a weapon or make threats; he scoops chips out of a bin into yellow baskets.

The chick at the gas station counter skims the till; her extroverted and inquisitive questions indicate that she's getting braver and greedier. She tosses my change onto the counter, ignoring my outstretched hand, and snorts, "I just can't keep money in my hands, falls through like water."

A man with red hair passes me in the parking lot, his mouth tightened with rage. He tries to contain himself, but I can't blame him; without consulting her husband, his wife recently invested their entire savings into a bunk business deal.

⁌

I don't always see clearly into people, more like a hazy flicker. I mentioned this debatable gift to a co-worker at the post office. I minimize, revealing just that I get 'vibes.' Velma and I speculate on the customers who come in to mail packages. This one eats Spam and calls his mother every other night. That one drove a VW Bug in college when he was free, but his new wife doesn't want to know about his past, just wants him to keep the SUV clean and the checks coming in. One lady buys clothes at Goodwill, but pretends they're from Macy's, another hires younger men for massages and kids herself that they really enjoy her company. Our stories are for our own pleasure, to laugh, to pass the time, to make the job more interesting. Velma doesn't know that I see many of these attributes.

⁓

My brother's new girlfriend is coming over tonight. I don't want to meet her. He doesn't really want me to meet her either, because I'm usually cold and rude to his dates. On the other hand, he wants me to like them, so he brings one around now and then. Since we live together, he always lets me know if anyone is stopping by. The last date had herpes. The one before was molested at age four by several uncles. One girl, fixated with money, would have emptied my brother's account in no time. Another hated men, but wanted to make her girlfriend jealous. My bother confirmed the molested girl and my neighbor knew the money-hungry one. The rest I'll probably never hear about.

⁓

The bank teller is cheating on her boyfriend with a man who wears silk shirts. She can't control herself because the obsession is unstoppable. The man next to me in line at the movies is dying of liver disease. The woman next to him doesn't know about his illness; they met online and this is only their third date. She's concerned that someone is following her, could be an ex-husband. No, an ex-boyfriend she also met online, a situation she regrets. She gave him too much of herself via the internet and when they met face-to-face, his neediness repulsed her. The woman behind me grieves over her dead husband. Her cousin next to her thinks a movie is the perfect grief-avoiding event, and loves to eat. She binges at night on pasta, taking huge bites.

⁓

I can't read everyone and I don't even know if I'm right most of the time. Perhaps my imagination is overactive? It's not like I can walk up to the girl at the ATM and ask, "Is it true that after you quit the San Francisco Ballet Company, you gained thirty pounds in four months and now avoid your dancing friends?" Or, could I approach the parking lot attendant and ask him to confirm that he spent one high-school summer on an aunt's farm in Kansas where he shot his first and only animal: a rabbit that lay dead, eyes opened, in a perfect curled pose, reminding him of a sleeping child?

I haven't told my brother about my ability. I almost did, but one day after I turned a corner, I bumped into someone. The man didn't say anything; he kept going. The way he tilted his chin toward his neck and looked wide-eyed toward the sky illustrated that he was a guilt-free rapist. At the time, he had never been caught and didn't plan to quit. His M.O. included offering rides to drunken girls who hung out at the lakefront. I stopped to watch him creep along the sidewalk as two police cars arrived out from the alley. Black-clad officials quietly arrested him. I read about him in the paper, the next day on the way to work. Scenarios of how my brother would react if I revealed my secret played in my head. But by the time the bus ride ended, I decided not to tell.

⤙

I whiz through the front door, pretending I'm in a hurry and jot right over to my room. I can hear my brother and the girl in the kitchen. He's using his I'm-charming-and-you-are-the-center-of-the-universe voice. She's giggling in that way girls do with guys they don't know well, a completely different giggle than if she was with girlfriends.

The interesting thing is, I can't read people until I see them, so I remain in my bedroom, listening.

He's enthralled. "You have the smoothest skin."

She protests, "No, I don't." Giggle.

He sniffs. "Mmm. And you smell so good."

The other weird thing is that I typically can't read people I know. Only strangers. So even if I entered the room, I wouldn't feel anything from my brother. But then again, maybe I don't need to. I already know him well enough.

Even though I didn't plan to meet her, I'm curious. It's hard for a woman in her own house to avoid checking out a strange woman in the other room. I enter the kitchen. She's sitting on our counter. Her skin does appear smooth. Her black hair looks Egyptian in that straight bang way.

"Hey, this is my sister."

"Nice to meet you." We shake hands.

In the span of time between his introduction and my response, I see that she wants to know what it is like to date an older man, because all the men her age have turned out to be scum. I'd say they're ten years different. Her ex-boyfriend slept over two months ago while his new girlfriend was out of town. She naively hopes her ex will come back, but knows and doesn't want to accept that he just came over to make sure he wasn't missing anything. She wants to find a good guy, but barely clings to the notion that one might be out there. If my brother doesn't work out, or if a man with good morals doesn't come into her life soon, she's afraid she'll slide into a jaded depression, or worse, her honesty might sour and she'll join the marching crowd of ruthlessness.

"Your kitchen is huge. Makes me want to cook." As she compliments us about our house, I understand that she's pregnant and doesn't know it.

My brother and the Egyptian chick look at me oddly. I should be answering them, but I can't yet. This is the first time I've known of someone unaware of their own pregnancy. That could mean that I'm catching the vibe of the unborn baby. I stare down at her stomach and try to capture more. The baby is content, but his skull has too much fluid and his heart is struggling.

The girl looks down at her belly because I am staring at it. "What?" She looks at my brother for support.

He squints at me. "You okay?"

I tell them, "I'm fine, just thinking," even though I'm not fine at all. The girl has a sweet integrity I don't often see. She struggles with the smallest fib.

I reach into my pocket and pull out my check stub. "Payday. How about I take us to dinner? To celebrate your new friendship."

The girl's shoulders drop in relief. Her eyes are grateful that I've welcomed her.

My brother relaxes, amazed; he thinks I finally approve of a date.

He opens the door for us and we all walk through.

THE WAY TO NOONIE'S

The even breathing—*ee-ee-aw ee-ee-aw*—of the machine sucked milk spurts into faded pink bottles. Noonie Wakehorn spent the rainy morning at home, as she had all week—pumping her breasts every fifteen minutes. When the white splashes retreated into dribbles, she kicked off the switch with her socked toe.

In between pumping, she checked her text messages. NO ND N SIGHT—from Mary Lou Stubbs, a fellow union worker sent to pace the strike lines because of her zero-production status, due to mastitis. And then another Mary Lou message: SM SHT DFF DAY.

Noonie found room in the over-stuffed freezer for the packets she labeled 'breast milk, 5 oz.' She hooked back up to the machine before her breasts ached too much, slumping and ignoring the cat rubbing at her ankle. The machine again. *Ee-ee-aw, ee-ee-aw,* like an old asthmatic.

At the next break, she reluctantly read her faxes that had slipped onto the floor: *Local 365 Wet Nurse Strike Continues—Still No Negotiation.* As she ripped and threw the paper toward the recycle basket, her eyes welled with tears. She missed her babies, her usual line-up in the mornings. Their coos, their tiny fingers playing with her braid while they suckled, their sighs, their perfect baby skin.

The union strike handbook said this would happen. "Emotional instability can result from infant withdrawal. Know that this is normal. Call the twenty-four hour strike support hotline if symptoms become severe." Gusts of hormones flowed when without the infants, even though Noonie pumped to keep the milk flowing and the ducts from clogging.

As she returned from the bathroom and unlatched her bra—she didn't even bother wearing a shirt these last few days, just a bra for support—a text from Mary Lou again—PUMP THIS.

The unused milk would make for a good quick profit, that is if the union could negotiate back pay for all the days out of the clinic. Otherwise, Noonie would have to pay rent with the precious frozen commodity. Either way, she hated looking into the freezer, rows and rows of plastic dated milk bags, like ice-covered soldiers unable to battle.

A sharp knock startled Noonie. She wiped her eyes, adjusted her breast pads, threw on a shirt, and opened the door. Rita Vitroncelli, one of the regular mothers from the clinic stood in the dripping rain while jiggling her wailing infant, Leonardo. "Noonie, you must help me." Rita pushed past into the living room.

Noonie left the door open and tried to usher Rita back outside. "I can't! We're striking and under contract." As Leonardo cried and squawked, as his bottom lip turned out and trembled, Noonie's breasts began to leak, the left more than the right, as usual. "I could get in huge trouble for having you in my home." She covered her breasts with a blanket as they'd begun to wet the shirt despite the pads. "I would lose my standing in the union and I'd lose my job."

Rita pleaded. "I just can't start him on formula. I'm out of stored milk. What about his immune system? His allergies?"

Noonie acknowledged to herself: how strange to have a customer in her own home. Although, of all her customers, Rita, who had gone through a double mastectomy and legitimately couldn't breastfeed, was one of the most endearing and appreciative of the mothers. If she had to have a customer in her house, it would be Rita rather than one of the mothers who'd leave their babies at the clinic—what Mary Lou called 'the drop and shop.' "How did you find me?"

Rita whispered as if someone might overhear, "Leonardo led me here."

Noonie's breasts pinched. She was not only behind schedule; Leonardo's persistent cries made her glands hard and painful.

Rita bounced wriggling Leonardo. "This morning, at the time I usually take him to the clinic to see you, he began to squeal. I had run out of your stored milk, the night-time milk, so I gave him water."

The women paused and shook their heads. Water indicated desperation.

Rita raised her voice above Leonardo's red-faced wailing. "Finally at ten this morning, I couldn't take it anymore. I put him in the car, hoping he'd fall asleep in his car seat, but he screeched non-stop, until I got on Santa Maria Drive, then he quieted. But, when I turned on North, he screamed again. So, I took a right on Pilgrim and he quieted. Every time he squealed, I'd turn again until he'd calm. I followed this pattern until he led me here. I drove past several times; he'd settle down right at your house. When I read the mailbox—Wakehorn—I knew it was you."

Leonardo reached his clenched fists toward Noonie. Tears streamed from his squeezed little eyes. He held his breath and turned dark purple.

"Please, just hold him. He needs you." Rita thrust the swaddled infant toward Noonie, who accepted the squirming package. "This is hard on all of us." Rita patted Noonie's arm. Leonardo turned his head and rooted around open-mouthed for Noonie's milk.

The little bundle felt so good. So soft. So right. Noonie reached to lock the door, lifted her shirt giving him the right nipple, the one he usually preferred. Leonardo latched and suckled. The room was instantly silent except for his audible swallows. Milk pooled in the corner of his mouth.

Rita always stayed with Leonardo. She never did a 'dump and pump'—what Mary Lou called mothers who went through the clinic drive thru. Now Rita caressed his head. "That's right, my Leo, that's right. It's all right now."

The two women moved to the couch. Rita adjusted pillows beneath Noonie's arm with one hand, with the other she stroked Leonardo's cheek. The baby slowed his sucking and with big clear eyes looked back and forth between mother and nurse. He gurgled, announcing a modest "Mmm" with every swallow.

Just like she did at the clinic, rather than giving him to one of the Burp Techs, Rita insisted on burping Leonardo herself, and after a good belch, handed the baby back to Noonie. "I'd give anything to do this myself," Rita whispered to Noonie who responded, "I know you would."

Leonardo's wee little fingers toyed with Noonie's braid while the hushed women watched him, instead of each other, and the rain drizzled on. *"Mmm. Mmm Mmm."*

THEY LEFT US DANGLING

In his pajamas, Miles announces the temperature, dew point and barometric pressure. He remains at an angle, somberly facing the window. Fidgeting with my hospital bracelet, I scrutinize his harshly pale feet; if he ran outside, those unsmiling ankles would be sallow stubs, vulnerable, merging with the snow.

In ten minutes, Bale will be buzzed in. Disgust will plug up her eyes when she sees the pajamas, and Miles will be hauled away to put on clothes. The morning routine: Miles protests, Bale insists, we hold down our cards and watch. Bale never hurts anyone, but the abruptness in her voice makes me think she's right on the edge of it.

I learned how to shuffle cards here. I'm unsure what else I'm supposed to learn, but yesterday, one of the counselors suggested each of us take a team member aside and discuss our goals. This should be on our own terms; the initiative will indicate our development. Dr. Shedley nodded at this proposition, clapped enthusiastically. I skipped joining in on the clap. Instead, I took the initiative to sneak one of Miles' smelly shoes to place it next to Fat Martha.

Viceroy sits across from me. I'm confused about him. Occasionally, he aggravates me. Most times, I look at Vice and want to lean against him. Or even be him. He maneuvers his body evenly, as if a current fluidly designs his movements. Maybe I'm jealous; he doesn't have useless breasts leading him around. It's not fair: men are just naturally muscular, but they barely have to work out.

Two aces rest in my left hand, I'm certain Vice holds two also, but he's trying to play it cool. The dumb asses in this game don't concentrate like Vice and me. You have to keep your eye on card travel if you want to win, at least if you wish to beat someone in particular.

Today, I need to defeat Vice; his ridiculous mouth opens and closes as if he's whispering. I want to pinch his lips. Instead, because Dr. Shedley indicated that I must find a healthy way to vent my frustration, I will pummel Vice in a card game.

With her scarred arm, Angie reaches across to grab a card. The welts from a grill, criss-cross, branding her like a steer. On my first day, she crept behind me, whispered that she was hiding a razor blade. Because I was new and shocked, I revealed this to Dr. Shedley, and they strip-searched Angie. I thought she'd be angry, but instead she appeared blank. They explained later that she pulls that stunt with all the new patients.

As Angie picks up her card, she palms one under. Uncertain of what to say, and amazed by her conspicuous attempt to cheat, I hold my breath. Vice seizes her wrist, hard enough to make the skin turn white around his nails. We stare at those nails, knowing that the game is over, but not sure what happens next. A low growl starts in Angie's throat and out come a couple of barks. She sounds like a puppy. I almost laugh until Vice puts her wrist in his mouth and chomps.

Wrestling, Viceroy and Angie knock the table over. On their way down, Vice's head smacks against the concrete pole; I flinch. The head smack seems worse than the wrist bite. Even though Vice's lips piss me off, at least he's honest. Angie's sneakiness is creepy, so I quietly cheer for Vice. Fighting is brief around here—the aides break up the commotion immediately—but scuffling sure does highlight the day. Angie and Vice are sent to lockdown. The rest of us gather the cards. I try to put them in order, but two of the aces are missing.

During the drama, I forgot about Miles. Miles is as aggravating as a dripping faucet, but if he's absent, I kind of miss his chatter. His pasty ankles shiver below the curtain, he must be frightened. As I shift closer, I can hear him mumbling about the wind chill factor and southwesterly knots. I gather a handful of curtain and pull it back. With his face to the wall, Miles trembles, appearing small and inept. The door buzzes, and here's Bale. I jump away and let her deal with Miles. It's almost time to eat anyway.

At the square breakfast table, Vice's, Angie's, and Miles' spots are empty. Only ten of us now. Usually it's Vice who is talkative; he tends to divulge details of his fights, until Bale or one of the other counselors reroutes the discussion. So now we're quiet, avoiding eyes. I'm hoping someone talks; it's not going to be me.

The shadow of Velvetta sits to my right; she's the one who will be last at the table, guaran-damn-teed. One time, Vice couldn't endure watching Velvetta eat so unbearably slow, either that or he was just feeling feisty. His fist slammed onto her hand while she held a spoon of bran cereal. That bran slop flew and landed on Bale's collar. They cancelled movie night because we laughed so hard. Bale's lame, she should have realized it was funny. Isn't laughter expected to help depressed patients?

Miles, with bed hair projecting like a car antenna, hesitates in the doorway. Bale forbids Miles from wearing his pajamas, but ignores his hair. Bale should be a patient here, she's acquired so many hangups. One guy starts in on Miles, asks him if his hairdo went through a jet stream. The counselors, keyed up after the Vice-Angie squabble, have little tolerance for stupidity. The smart-ass is sent to his room. I have zero sympathy; we know we're not to encourage Miles to talk about the weather.

I pick at my bran cereal, but wish for some pancakes, ice cream, and cookie dough. Always bran for breakfast for those of us on meds; helps the flow. At least we receive a banana today which I scarf down in three bites.

Bale, with her sweaty forehead, follows me to my room, parks her annoying self in my doorway and asks what I know about this morning's episode as I urinate. I was busy playing cards, didn't notice much. I've concluded the best position is to stay neutral around here; some folks aren't real stable.

Bale discloses that the team is indecisive about our walk tonight. There's snow due this afternoon and everyone seems to be misbehaving today. On the other hand, she thinks fresh air would be good; we've been cramped indoors for two weeks.

I strive to ignore her, I despise her so much. Anyone that would take a job following bulimics to the bathroom is crazier than I am. I disbelieve her story about going out or staying in; she said it to make me anxious.

Last week, I ditched her while she sat with Velvetta. I barfed the bran cereal and rammed in fifty-five sit-ups before she checked on me. Pulling one over on Sweaty Forehead Bale was thrilling, but I hadn't puked in sixty-two days. I felt really low after blowing it.

I used to be embarrassed going in front of Bale, but now, since I have no respect for her, I think it's sickening. I stride past, she searches my face; I know she's looking for evidence of successful provocation, but I'm expressionless. I snatch my towel and sprint to find my shower partner, Fat Martha. Bale follows behind.

I discover Fat Martha in the kitchen with Velvetta. Fat Martha, who received word directly from God to consume as much as possible, thinks she's helping by trying to persuade Velvetta to finish breakfast.

Maybe Bale considers this a good idea, but I have an eating disorder and know much better; fat people will not convince an anorexic to eat, in fact, after viewing Fat Martha's rolls, Velvetta may never eat again. Velvetta is an eighty-nine-pound skeleton with a hint of skin. She was my shower partner for the first week; I tried not to look at her angling bones, her caved in stomach. At the same time, I'd sneak glimpses.

Velvetta slumps, choking on slow babyish tears. Why cry? Why make an event after every meal? Why waste everyone's time? She captures a lot of attention; I guess that's what she wants. Not me, I wish they'd just leave me the hell alone. That's the thing about this place: there are patients, patients who think they should be counselors, or counselors who should be patients.

Fat Martha ogles Velvetta's cereal; I tell her to knock it off, it's shower time. She squints at me, even her eyelids are chubby. I don't care how she glares at me. She's huge. I'd kill myself before I got that large.

In the shower, I avoid the sight of Fat Martha. If I accidentally get a peek, the vision makes me double the pace of my jogging. Martha can't tell them about my workout routine in the shower, because if she does, I'll let loose about the candy her pastor brings every Thursday when he comes to pray with her. His Holy Dimness believes she's been touched divinely; she merely wants the candy.

In the dressing room, I alternate twenty bends between each article of clothing. Fat Martha blathers on about how Vice should get kicked out for biting Angie. I don't think the counselors saw the bite; I hope not. Even though Vice's habit of moving his lips annoys me, I'd hate for him to leave. He's the only one with any intelligence around here. Until Vice and I pleaded for some classics, we suffered with a lone shelf of poorly written, non-violent, non-sexual mystery novels, handpicked by a nun, no doubt. Besides, I like to watch him. When he squats to view the bottom shelf or reaches across in ping-pong, his movements are effortless and uncomplicated.

Twenty pushups before brushing my teeth, thirty jumping jacks after flossing. Fat Martha slathers oil on her wobbly arms. On my ninth pull-up on the shower curtain rod, Angie walks in without a shower partner. Her entrance blows my workout; sit-ups were next.

I'm afraid to ask how she got out of lockup so soon; that would require connection with her empty eyes. Last time our eyes met, an uneasy feeling jarred me enough to feel nauseous. It was an ugly re-action, like opening up the trash, only to find maggots.

Bale confided that Angie was incessantly beaten by her now im-prisoned stepdad. Knowing still didn't make me feel sorry for Angie much; she's hatred personified, how can I feel compassionate? Fat Martha and I bunch up our stuff and almost run for the door.

·⤺

After dinner, we wait for Group in the dayroom. Vice still hasn't joined us. Two of the guys playing ping-pong ask Miles if it's go-ing to snow tonight. One of them is so dumb, he is lucky to be alive; the other is just an idiot. They should wish they had Miles' smarts. It's just too bad Miles is stuck on one subject. "Thunderstorms with damaging winds, large hail, and a few tornadoes across the Midwest."

I start to sink slowly into a puffy chair, but hover above it. Squatting gives the quadriceps such a good burn. Then, in the chair, I sit up and back twenty-five times, clenching my stomach muscles. Bale catches me and tells me to quit it. Watching the window, I act as if I don't know what she's talking about.

Bale rushes out of this building every night at five; the lake air blasts her face when she opens the door; then she travels wherever she pleases. She gets to eat whatever she wants without worrying about her weight. She gets to run ten miles if she wants to. What are twenty-five sit-ups to her? I have nowhere to go for exercise. And no fresh air. I'm atrophying; this stupid body is getting flabbier every second. Pushing my hands together, I accomplish some isometrics.

Vice shows up late for Group. He's subdued, but catches my eye and shrugs. He's kind of good looking in a windswept sort of way. Dr. Shedley wants us to talk about this morning's card game and how to deal with conflict. I know exactly: you shove it in your head and walk away. You swallow discomfort and harbor pain.

The possibility that I could bite someone or hit them, even if I wanted to, was always beyond inappropriate. Violence, not only unacceptable, was unattainable. Unlike Vice, I'm a person who hides, who dwells instead of punches.

Dr. Shedley encourages us to be *assertive,* "Stand up for yourself and speak your mind." He says this as if it's as easy as ordering fries at a drive-up window. "Basically, too much anger will do one of two things: accumulate, then burst like an overinflated raft, or implode and take your mind with it." His hands grab the space around him, draws it in toward his gut.

I hadn't realized there were options, for me at least. Perhaps there are two things I've learned in this damn hospital: how to shuffle, and an understanding that instead of possessing an imploding mind, I could go the other way, I could be violent. It wouldn't be the end of the world if I fought someone; I'd still get invited to Group.

Bale darts into the room, then stops, trying to appear natural. Dr. Shedley glances up, ignoring Velvetta drag on about her status of victim in today's society of fashion worship. I agree with her about our culture's obsession with thinness, but hope I express myself with fewer whines. Dr. Shedley excuses himself and whispers with Bale. The only word I hear is 'Angie.'

Everyone in Group starts yakking now that we're leaderless, but I detect the two slip out the door in a hurry. Vice watches too. For the first time, our group is unaccompanied—dangling.

Vice rises. A few sit back to stay out of his way. He tugs my arm lightly until I stand. He searches my eyes. The solid grip on my arm startles me; it's been months since I've been touched. His lips are still. I don't know what he wants, but I feel curious, though logically, I should be disturbed.

He sweeps hair from my eyes while scrutinizing me with a look of amused approval. "Okay?" he asks. A brave and reckless feeling bubbles up from my stomach and I feel like laughing. I smile hugely. "Okay," I say because I know what he means now, and I don't care if it's wrong, this opportunity will never happen again.

Smelling like pine, he leans forward, close to my face. I'm reminded of a forceful sky before a storm. He kisses me. He starts soft. We're gentle as if testing each other's strength, until I dig my fingers into his back muscles and pull him in.

Astonishment and hooting pours from our hospital mates. His hands roughly grasp my hair, forcing me even closer. My teeth hold his lower lip, then I slowly ease the pressure, teasing back into the kiss.

A brimming sensation rises from my insides. Someone whoops. If feelings have color, this one would be the brown-red of almost burnt toast. The Group roars up with cheers.

Breathless we part, just before Dr. Shedley dashes in, bewildered and frantic, his dark hair flopping like a wet dress sock, "What's wrong?"

What a question, Dr. Shedley. Indeed, what a question for us.

Hugging himself like he's chilled, Vice leans back into his chair, eyes closed. Miles, rocking back and forth, mumbles, "Scattered clouds, chance of snow on Tuesday." Fat Martha swallows a Tootsie Roll.

Forgetting to squat slowly, I plop into my puffy chair. I trace my lips with my fingers and kick my legs over the side to let them swing.

THE SEVEN YEAR-OLD

The seven year-old asks me, "Could you please lay down your baby, so I can dissect him?" I say, *No, he's been dissected twice today. He's tired of it.*

·

The seven year-old runs to his closet and returns with a red cape. "Could you please drop your baby from the roof so I can rescue him just before he hits the ground?" I say, *No, I don't want him to assume someone will always be there to catch him.*

·

The seven year-old asks if he can please stab my infant with his white sword. I say, *No, impalement is not becoming on a baby. He will have trouble digesting his food.*

·

The seven year-old dons a feathered hat to go with the cape. "Could you then run toward me like a bull?" I say, *yes,* and race toward him with the baby under my arm. For a moment we are lost in the cape of the bullfighter. He takes the cape away, and it makes us angry. *Give us back that red!* We charge again and again and again.

PRIESTS AND BALLOONS

The priest can no longer look into his maid's eyes. He used to be able to ask for tea, another biscuit, even a change of bed linens. Now, as she serves him a piece of their son's birthday cake, Father Rutkowski murmurs *thank you* and pats the child's head, the child who doesn't know his father as a father, but as a Father. "Happy birthday, my son."

Adelle whispers in his ear and for a brief moment, he thinks he can feel her swelling belly on his arm, "He looks just like you today."

She smells of bravery and frosting.

The child hands him three balloons, two blues and a yellow. Father Rutkowski's chest doesn't seem so leaden. "Hand me more."

The boy runs throughout the party snatching strings from little hands. He unties knots from the backs of chairs. Reds, purples, a white.

"Please fetch *all* the balloons, son," the priest says to the giggling child.

With each colorful delivery, the priest's neck loosens; the taut muscles along his spine relax.

Finally, every last balloon bouquets the Father.

While the maid turns her back to wipe the mouth of a toddler, the priest allows himself to ascend. He wavers for a moment along the ceiling, looking down on cherubic faces.

Father Rutkowski, someday a grandfather, glides out the window.

BREATHING OYSTERS

S he names her new dog Molecule after the neighbor, a bio-tech engineer, names his dog Molecule. She is always doing things like that, replicating someone else's brainy idea. Her boyfriend brings this up, "Just like when you lined the drive with tiki torches, identical to your dad's." She says she thought of it first.

He mentions the camping trip, why he wasn't shocked when they ended up at Hendy Woods, just like her sister. "This is getting creepy. I can't even buy clothes anymore." He reminds her of their matching toothbrushes, ski pants, deerskin slippers, silk long underwear, Gortex rain jackets. He says he is leaving, Molecule is the last straw, but not until after the oysters. "I'm not wasting good bar-bequed oysters."

They are in bed when he announces his departure. She clings on his arm like a pasted barnacle. "I'm leaving too," she wails.

"You can't leave. I'm leaving," he shrugs her off. "Quit copying me."

She runs her tongue along his forearm. "Maybe the oysters will change your mind."

"We have to eat them before they die."

She presses her nose on his. "They're alive?"

He presses back. "When they're cooked and officially dead, they crack open."

Molecule gets between them, licking each face back and forth.

"Your dog has nasty breath."

"Please don't go."

"If you name him something else, if you dye your hair a different color than Double Espresso #47—my mother's color—if you sell your Jeep—the identical Jeep my brother drives—if you swear to never ever buy one thing that I already own, I will consider staying."

There is a lot of silence. She thinks she can hear the dozen oysters moving in the refrigerator. She is used to just the two of them, now the two of them plus dog, breathing in her house. "I can hear them breathe."

"Who?"

"The oysters."

"Name him Oyster." He rolls on top of her, pins down her shoulders. "Name him Oyster or I will be gone tomorrow."

"But that is your idea." She maneuvers a leg across him and pushes him away with a foot to a chin.

"So what." He bashes her with a pillow. "I gave you permission."

She throws a pillow back and then a lamp. "I don't like the name Oyster."

"You don't know what you like." He pulls the belt out of his pants and holds it in front of her face. "Oyster."

She pinches both his nipples. "Molecule."

He snaps the belt, puts it behind her, and draws her in to him, tight. They are naked except for matching blue Fruit-of-the-Loom men's briefs.

"Molecule," she whispers.

He pulls her in tighter, fastening the belt around both their necks. He holds her hands behind her back. "Oyster."

"Molecule."

He grips her wrists with one fist and blows into her ear. "Oy?"

She bites a mouthful of his hair. "Ster."

There is no more discussion about it, but he doesn't let go. She listens closely, hears twelve gasps from the refrigerator and uncountable breaths elsewhere.

DOUBLE UNDIE NIGHT

Because her husband doesn't come home until 3 A.M., she shoots him with pepper spray.

He is drunk and believes her when she apologizes, saying she thought the *bang-crumple-crumple* on the screen door was the horrifying sound of an intruder.

"Sorry, hon," she dabs his face with a wet washcloth.

He wavers in the bedroom, closed-eyed and wobbly, "Why do they make pants so difficult?"

She doesn't help him undress, but instead pours water in his boots.

As he pulls on a second pair of underwear over the first, she feels almost compelled to tell him of his error, but instead offers to make a sandwich. Tomato and cream cheese on one half, chopped cucumber and cat litter sprinkle the other.

He squints as he chomps.

"Crunchy bread. Lots of sourdough seeds." She places a glass of milk next to his relaxed hand. "To bed with me."

"I love *you.*" He sprays food across the table. "You're the one. I tell *everybody.*"

She snuggles into the sheets and listens to him bumble around in the dining room. "Why so many chairs?"

He bomb-flops onto his side of the bed with the gasoline gush of beer stink.

She waits for that even huff-breath before she removes his foot from the covers. He snores as she uncaps the bottle of Sweet Magenta Sky nail polish. She starts with the big toe, bulbous compared to the rest, one slow stroke at a time.

EVERY GIRL HAS AN EX NAMED STEVE

We tell her not to date a man in a banana suit. A boy, really. She's young and doesn't know any better, but dang, we wish she'd listen to our advice. We're years older, we've been through it all, we know better. We tell her this on her bed, we six sisters, we six girls, quietly, so Dad doesn't hear. If he only knew his oops-from-a-second-marriage-homeschooled-protected-youngest had the hotsies over a banana.

We're not going to tell him.

We point out the guy's feet. *They are splayed,* we say, *duck-like. Quack, quack,* we say. She loves his feet, they show vulnerability. We are concerned about his eyes. They remind us of an alien in an after school special, who just wanted to be human and loved.

Loved, she says, her face reddening.

We look at each other in silence. She's doomed. She said, *loved.* The oldest sister points out that being a banana at Jamba Juice isn't a career; he doesn't even know what he wants in life. But, the lovebird says she doesn't care, she loves the way he says *Razzamataz.* She repeats it. We repeat it. *Razzamataz?* It is the name of the smoothie she always orders.

What is his name? someone finally asks, and we all say, *Yeah, what is his name anyway?*

Steve. She says Steve as if she is plucking the first ripe peach off a summer tree.

Steve? We push and shove each other. *Didn't you date a Steve? And you?*

We come to the conclusion we've all had Bad Steves. At least six Bad Steves—including one ex-husband Steve—and one more, a not-really-dated Bad Steve that stood up the second eldest at the drive-thru A&W. Extra embarrassing because she had to call Dad to come get her. There was no way the standing-up-Steve could have redeemed himself after Dad got involved.

Our banana-enthralled-virgin is fussing with the corner of her pink spread. She is trembling a bit, and one sister says, *Don't cry, this might be the Steve exception.* We all pat her and apologize. *There are always anomalies,* we say, and the sister who is a scientist explains that in nature there are occasionally mutations that breed into something extraordinary. She says, *For instance, look at the . . .*

Dad opens the door. *Girls! This is dangerous. You're all in one room.*

Come in, we all say.

I might get swallowed alive, he says. He sits on the edge of the bed next to the lip-quiverer and pats her head. *Love talk?*

The tears burst out. Dad has the way of doing that.

The banana?

How did you know? we all ask.

He lifts up her chin, *It's the way he says Razzamataz, isn't it?* He's trying not to smile and so are we. Two sisters have to leave the room.

The four of us gather around Dad and the little one, holding her while she sobs, *And, his name is Steve. Why does his name a have to be Steve?*

Unfortunately, some guys are just like that, Dad says.

ABOUT THE AUTHOR

Stefanie Freele was born and raised in Wisconsin. She currently lives in the Pacific Northwest; she soon hopes to build a cabin with her family on their property near Sandpoint, Idaho.

Her short fiction has appeared or is forthcoming in many magazines, including *Glimmer Train, American Literary Review, Night Train, Literary Mama, McSweeney's Internet Tendency, Westview, Talking River* and *Hobart*.

After receiving the Kathy Fish Fellowship and serving as the 2008 Writer In Residence for *SmokeLong Quarterly*, she joined their editorial staff. Ms. Freele is also Fiction Editor of the *Los Angeles Review*. She has an MFA from the Northwest Institute of Literary Arts: Whidbey Writers Workshop.